BENIGHT

JOHN BOYNTON PRIESTLEY was born in
schoolmaster. After leaving Belle Vue Sch
in a wool office but was already by this
writer. He volunteered for the army in 1914 during the First World War
and served five years; on his return home, he attended university and
wrote articles for the *Yorkshire Observer*. After graduating, he established
himself in London, writing essays, reviews, and other nonfiction, and
publishing several miscellaneous volumes. In 1927 his first two novels
appeared, *Adam in Moonshine* and *Benighted*. In 1929 Priestley scored his
first major critical success as a novelist, winning the James Tait Black
Memorial Prize for *The Good Companions*. *Angel Pavement* (1930) followed
and was also extremely successful. Throughout the next several decades,
Priestley published numerous novels, many of them very popular and
successful, including *Bright Day* (1946) and *Lost Empires* (1965), and was
also a prolific and highly regarded playwright.

Priestley died in 1984, and though his plays have continued to be
published and performed since his death, much of his fiction has
unfortunately fallen into obscurity. Valancourt Books is in the process of
reprinting many of J. B. Priestley's best works of fiction with the aim of
allowing a new generation of readers to discover this unjustly neglected
author's books.

FICTION BY J.B. PRIESTLEY

Adam in Moonshine (1927)

Benighted (1927)*

Farthing Hall (with Hugh Walpole) (1929)

The Good Companions (1929)

Angel Pavement (1930)

Faraway (1932)

Wonder Hero (1933)

I'll Tell You Everything (with Gerald Bullett) (1933)

They Walk in the City (1936)

The Doomsday Men (1938)*

Let the People Sing (1939)

Blackout in Gretley (1942)

Daylight on Saturday (1943)

Three Men in New Suits (1945)

Bright Day (1946)

Jenny Villiers (1947)

Festival at Farbridge (1951)

The Other Place (1953)*

The Magicians (1954)*

Low Notes on a High Level (1954)

Saturn Over the Water (1961)*

The Thirty First of June (1961)*

The Shapes of Sleep (1962)*

Sir Michael and Sir George (1964)

Lost Empires (1965)

Salt is Leaving (1966)*

It's an Old Country (1967)

The Image Men: Out of Town (vol. 1), *London End* (vol. 2) (1968)

The Carfitt Crisis (1975)

Found Lost Found (1976)

* Available from Valancourt Books

J. B. Priestley

BENIGHTED

*. . . . . the bright day is done,
And we are for the dark. . . . .*

With an introduction by
ORRIN GREY

VALANCOURT BOOKS

Benighted by J. B. Priestley
First published London: Heinemann, 1927
Original U.S. title: *The Old Dark House*
First Valancourt Books edition 2013, reprinted 2018

Published by Valancourt Books, Richmond, Virginia
http://www.valancourtbooks.com

ISBN 978-1-948405-09-6 (*trade paperback*)
ISBN 978-1-948405-10-2 (*hardcover*)

Also available as an electronic book and an audiobook.

All Valancourt Books publications are printed on acid free paper that
meets all ANSI standards for archival quality paper.

Cover by Henry Petrides
Set in Dante MT

INTRODUCTION

In 1927, a 33-year-old Englishman named John Boynton (J. B.) Priestley published his first two novels, *Adam in Moonshine* and *Benighted*. For many readers who are picking up *Benighted* for the first time, however, it won't be the novel itself that led them here. While the book was quite popular upon its release, and while Priestley went on to great success as a novelist, dramatist, and screenwriter, it is the cinematic version of *Benighted* that most people know today, if they know it at all, and it would be impossible to write an introduction to the book without first talking a little bit about the film.

Priestley's novel was released in the United States in 1928 under the title *The Old Dark House*, which immediately positioned it as a deconstruction or summation of 'old dark house' stories, a popular subgenre at the time. (In much the same way, Joss Whedon and Drew Goddard would use the title of their 2011 film *The Cabin in the Woods* to signal their intentions toward that unofficial subgenre.) Old dark house stories featured groups of eclectic strangers gathering at some secluded house for the reading of a will, say, or stranded there when the bridge washes out in a rainstorm. They were extremely popular in the theater of the 1920s, and then on the screens of silent cinema, and even into the 'talkies' of the 1930s and 1940s. Some of the most popular examples include *The Bat* and *The Cat and the Canary*, both of which found life on screen multiple times over the years. To modern audiences, the genre may be best known for its parody in the cult hit *The Rocky Horror Picture Show*.

The first film version of Priestley's *The Old Dark House* was released by Universal Pictures in 1932, and was seen by many (then and later) as the 'apotheosis of all "old house" chillers', as William K. Everson would put it in his 1974 book *Classics of the Horror Film*. Directed by the legendary James Whale, its release is sandwiched between his more famous films *Frankenstein* (1931), *The Invisible Man* (1933), and *Bride of Frankenstein* (1935). The cast of *The Old Dark House* is composed of a who's who of James Whale favorites, including Ernest Thesiger (Dr. Pretorius in *Bride of Frankenstein*) and Gloria Stuart (*The Invisible Man*), as well as Boris Karloff, who gets a special note in the credits assuring viewers that he is the same actor who played Frankenstein's monster the year before, 'to settle all disputes in advance'. The rest of the incredible ensemble cast is rounded out by names like Melvyn Douglas, Charles Laughton, and Lilian Bond.

The Old Dark House wasn't considered a big success for Universal upon its release in the United States, though it broke box office records in the U.K. It was shelved shortly after its production and Universal let the rights lapse in 1957. In spite of an unrecognizable William Castle remake in 1963, the original film wasn't seen again for decades and was considered a 'lost film' until a negative was discovered and restored thanks to the efforts of Curtis Harrington, director of 'classic' schlock films like *Queen of Blood* and *Whoever Slew Auntie Roo?*

Those who are coming to *Benighted* by way of *The Old Dark House* will find that the movie was a delightfully faithful reproduction of the book. Many of the film's best and most famous lines are taken wholesale from the novel, including Penderel's musing, 'Supposing the people inside were dead, all stretched out with the lights quietly burning about them', and Rebecca Femm's speech to Margaret about 'fine stuff, but it'll rot'. The film is funnier, and, in true Hollywood fashion, the ending is happier, though it wasn't always. The movie originally ended just as the book does, but it was re-shot after preview screenings determined that audiences wouldn't respond as well to the book's more tragic climax.

While *Benighted* is as preoccupied with the conventions of the old dark house genre as its cinematic counterpart, there are a lot of other things going on just beneath its mannered surface. Positioned between the two World Wars, the shadow of the first still lays heavy over the characters, while the specter of the second looms unspoken on the horizon. It is a time of tension, between hope and disillusionment, between the old world and the industrial age, between superstition and rationality. Beneath its veneer of charming suspense, the book captures the tension of all these dichotomies in the changing relationships of its characters, and in the conflict between the medieval Femm house and the more modern visitors forced to take shelter there from the storm outside.

Because the novel can get inside the heads of its characters in a way that is largely denied to film, *Benighted* has a more meditative quality and brings with it a sense of existential dread that *The Old Dark House* has largely replaced with more cinema-friendly bumps in the night. The dread is brought on partly by the aftermath of the war and its effects on the characters, and partly by the changing tides of modern life, but it also has elements of something else. Something older, that borders at times on the 'cosmic horror' that was practiced by writers like Algernon Blackwood, Arthur Machen, and H.P. Lovecraft, though its closer relation would probably be found in the works of Stephen Crane. This dread comes not from any human agency, but from the sense that the universe itself is not a rational thing, and that humanity's place within it is not an exalted one.

Though there are no monsters or supernatural phenomena in *Benighted*, there's a passage in the middle of the book that provides a nice summation of the novel's pervading sense of dread, but could just as easily serve as a primer for Lovecraft's brand of cosmic horror:

His mind, outracing him, found an opposing presence, an enemy, but no name for it; a density of evil, something gigantic, ancient but enduring, only dimly felt before, but now taking the mind by storm; it was working everywhere, in the mirk of rain outside, here in the rotting corners, and without end, in the black between the stars.

Though there is much humor to be had in *Benighted*, it is a humor always in the shadow of the gallows, a way of whistling past the graveyard. The book's mannered quality feels less like an old-fashioned theatricality and more like the characters are clinging to their manners as shields against an uncaring and chaotic universe, a fear as much of the uncertain future as the 'benighted' past.

Which all runs the risk of making *Benighted* sound a bit stuffy, when really it's anything but. One of the chief joys of the novel is in its ability to be read as a simple and enjoyable old dark house chiller just as easily as it can be mined for deeper thematic significance.

By the time the film version of *The Old Dark House* was released, Priestley had already become famous for the 1929 release of his third novel *The Good Companions*, which won him the James Tait Black Memorial Prize for fiction, and was itself filmed twice (once in 1933 and again in 1957). Priestley went on to write more than twenty additional novels, as well as numerous plays and short stories. He remained prolific until his death in 1984. The Internet Movie Database credits him as writer on more than 90 titles, many of them film versions of his various plays. His first play, *Dangerous Corner*, was adapted for film at least four times. Today, however, much of his fiction is unjustly neglected, and many of his best works are out of print. This Valancourt Books edition marks the first time that *Benighted* has been widely available in almost half a century. It's a momentous occasion for fans of the novel, or fans of the film, or anyone who enjoys a good 'old dark house' tale, especially one that has a little more substance than most.

ORRIN GREY

ORRIN GREY's stories of monsters, ghosts, and sometimes the ghosts of monsters have appeared in dozens of anthologies, including Ellen Datlow's *Best Horror of the Year*, and he is the author of the story collections *Never Bet the Devil & Other Warnings*, *Painted Monsters & Other Strange Beasts*, and *Guignol & Other Sardonic Tales*, as well as *Monsters from the Vault*, a collection of his essays on vintage horror cinema.

BENIGHTED

CHAPTER I

Margaret was saying something, but he couldn't hear a word. The downpour and the noise of the engine were almost deafening. Suddenly he stopped the car and leaned back, relieved, relaxed, free for a moment from the task of steering a way through the roaring darkness. He had always felt insecure driving at night, staring out at a little lighted patch of road and groping for levers and switches, pressing pedals, had always been rather surprised when the right thing happened. But to-night, on these twisting mountain roads, some of them already awash, with storm after storm bursting upon them and the whole night now one black torrent, every mile was a miracle. It couldn't last. Their rattling little box of mechanical tricks was nothing but a piece of impudence. He turned to Margaret.

'You needn't have done that,' she was saying now. She had had to raise her voice, of course, but it was as cool and clear as ever. She was still detached, but apparently, for once, not amused.

'Done what?' Philip returned, but his heart sank, for he knew what she meant. Then he felt annoyed. Couldn't he stop the damned thing for a minute? He was easily the coldest and wettest of the three of them.

'You needn't have stopped the car,' Margaret replied. 'I was only saying that we ought to have turned back before. It's simply idiotic going on like this. Where are we?'

He felt an icy trickle going down his back and shook himself.

'Hanged if I know,' he told her. 'Somewhere in wildest Wales. That's as near as I can get. I've never found my bearings since we missed that turning. But I think the direction's vaguely right.' He wriggled a little. He was even wetter than he had imagined. He had got wet when he had gone out to change the wheel and then later when she had stopped and he had had to look at the engine, and since then the rain had been coming in steadily. Not all the hoods and screens in the world could keep out this appalling downpour.

'This is hopeless.' Margaret was calmly condemning the situation. 'What time is it?'

There was no light on the dashboard, so he struck a match and held it near the clock. Half-past nine. There was just time to catch a glimpse of Margaret's profile before the tiny flame vanished. It was like overhearing a faintly scornful phrase about himself. He suddenly felt responsible for the whole situation, not only for the delay on the road and the missed turning, but for the savage hills and the black spouting night. Once again he saw himself fussing away, nervous, incompetent, slightly disordered, while she looked on, critical, detached, indulgent or contemptuous. When anything went wrong—and it was in the nature of things to go wrong—she always made him feel like that. Perhaps all wives did. It wasn't fair. It was taking a mean advantage of the fact that you cared what they thought, for once you stopped caring the trick must fail.

'We'd better go on and try and arrive somewhere,' Margaret was saying. 'Shall I drive now?' He was expecting that. She always imagined that she was the better driver. And perhaps she was, though. Not really so skilful with the wheel, the gears, the brakes, but far cooler than he was simply because she never saw the risks. Her imagination didn't take sudden leaps, didn't see a shattered spine a finger's breadth away, didn't realise that we all went capering along a razor-edge. Unlike him, she blandly trusted everything, everything, that is, except human beings. Now they were not so bad, merely stupid—the thought came flashing as he shifted his position—it was only the outside things that were so devilish.

'No, thanks. I'll keep on. There's no point in changing now. We'll arrive somewhere soon.' He was about to reach out to the switch when the light of a match at the back turned him round. Penderel, who had been dozing there for the last two hours, was now lighting a cigarette. 'Hello!' he shouted back. 'You all right, Penderel? Not drowned yet?' Penderel's face, queerly illuminated, looked at once drawn and impish. A queer stick!—mad as a hatter some people thought, Margaret among them; but Philip wasn't sure. He suddenly felt glad to see him there. Penderel wouldn't mind all this.

Penderel blew out smoke, held up the lighted match, and leaned forward, as vivid as a newly painted portrait. He grinned. 'Where are we?' Then the match went out and he was nothing but a shadow.

'We don't know,' Philip shouted back above the drumming rain. 'We've missed the way. We're somewhere in the Welsh mountains and it's half-past nine. Sorry.'

'Don't mention it.' Penderel seemed to be amused. 'I say, this storm's going on for ever. I believe it's the end of the world. They've overheard the talk at the Ainsleys and have decided to blot us all out. What do you think?'

Philip felt Margaret stirring beside him. He knew that her body was stiffening with disapproval, partly because the Ainsleys, with whom they had all three been staying, were old friends of hers, but chiefly because she didn't like Penderel, whose existence she had almost forgotten, and was only too ready to disapprove of everything he said or did. 'We shan't see even Shrewsbury to-night,' Philip shouted back. A halt at Shrewsbury had been their modified plan, following upon their delay on the road and their slow progress in the torrential rain.

'Shrewsbury!' Penderel laughed. 'Nor the Hesperides either. We'll be lucky if we get anywhere, out of this. I'll tell you what'—he hesitated a moment—'I don't want to frighten Mrs. Waverton——'

'Go on, Mr. Penderel.' Margaret was icy. 'I'm not easily frightened.'

'Aren't you? I am,' Penderel replied, loudly and cheerfully. He seemed to be for ever putting his foot in it, either didn't know or didn't care. 'I was thinking that you'll have to be careful here. We've had a week's heavy rain, and thunderstorms for the last two days, and in this part of the world they're always having landslides and whatnot. Don't be surprised to find yourself driving into the middle of a lake, or the whole hillside coming down on you, or the road disappearing under the front wheels.'

The noise and the darkness made snubbing difficult, but Margaret did what she could. 'I must say I should be very surprised indeed,' she threw back. 'Hurry on, Philip. Open the windscreen. We can't be any wetter than we are now and I want to look out for any turnings or signposts.'

'Not that I care, you know,' Penderel called out. 'I don't want to go to Shrewsbury. I don't particularly want to go anywhere. Something might happen here, and nothing ever happens in Shrewsbury, and nothing much on the other side of Shrewsbury. But here there's always a chance.'

As Philip started the car again he wished himself a hundred miles the other side of Shrewsbury, moving sedately down some sensible main road towards a fire and clean sheets. The road they were on now seemed little better than a track, twisting its way along the hillside. There were no lights to be seen, nothing but the flashing rain and the jumping scrap of lighted road ahead, full of deep ruts and stones and shining with water. He moved cautiously forward, shaking the raindrops from his eyes and gripping the wheel as hard as he could. This ring of metal seemed his only hold upon security now that everything was black and sliding and treacherous, and even then it rattled uselessly in his hand at times. One silly twist and they were bogged for the night or even over the edge. Earlier it had been rather exhilarating rushing through this savagery of earth and weather, but now he felt tired and apprehensive. Penderel had been exaggerating, of course, perhaps trying to frighten Margaret. But no, he wouldn't be doing that, though he probably knew that she didn't like him and was against his returning from the Ainsleys' with them. He exaggerated for his own good pleasure, being a wild youth who liked to see life as either a screaming buffoonery or a grand catastrophe, something Elizabethan in five acts. Yet there were landslides after heavy rain in this part of the world. There might be floods too. Philip saw them stuck somewhere on this hillside all night. And what a night too! He shivered and involuntarily pressed the accelerator.

The car roared forward, and though he immediately released the pressure it did not slacken speed because there was a sudden dip in the road. Just in front the hillside jutted into a sharp edge of rock and the road turned a blind corner. Philip had only time to touch the footbrake when this corner swung towards him. He gave the wheel a hard twist; for a second the car went sliding; and the next moment they were round the corner but apparently plunging into a river. The road had disappeared; there was nothing ahead but the gleam of water. In they went with a roar and a splash. Philip gripped the wheel harder than ever; he felt Margaret's hand upon his left arm; he heard a shout from Penderel behind. Then the roaring and splashing filled the night, but the car seemed to be slowing down. He accelerated and the engine responded with loud spasmodic bursts, but all to no purpose. The car swung forward, stopped, drummed, and then shook violently, swung forward again, then stopped.

'Don't stop.' Margaret was crying in his ear.

'Can't help it,' he shouted. What a damn silly remark! Did she think they were in a motor-boat! He must do something though. The engine was still running, trembling there under his feet, like a hunted beast. Hastily he shoved the lever into low gear and rammed down the accelerator. The car gave an agonised roar and seemed to shake itself like a dog, but for a moment or so nothing else happened. 'Here for the night, here for the night,' Philip heard himself chanting idiotically. Then slowly, almost painfully it seemed, the car moved forward, protesting every yard against the unfamiliar element. And now the road began to climb again; the worst was passed; the lights showed solid ground ahead, and a few minutes' more splashing brought them out into earth and air. The little box of tricks had won. At least, Philip reminded himself, it had won so far; end of first round. But what was coming next? They were still climbing a little, and now the hillside to the right seemed less steep and rocky, but that to the left fell away more sharply. He could see nothing there but rain falling into a black gulf. It had the curiously vivid and dramatic quality of rain in a film.

Margaret was saying something and appeared to be fumbling in the pocket in the door. What was it she wanted? He caught the word 'stop' in her reply, and so once again brought the car to a standstill. 'What is it?' he asked.

'I'm looking for the map,' she replied. 'We must find out where we are. We can't go on like this.'

'A good voyage, Waverton!' Penderel shouted. 'Have a cigarette?' Philip found the open case under his nose when he turned, and lit up with Penderel. Then there was a little click and the whole car was illuminated, transformed into a queer tiny room. The night was banished, wind and rain and darkness disappearing behind the shining screen; Margaret had found the little observation lamp and had fixed it in the plug. She had also found the map and was now bending over it, the lamp in her hand. But it was only a flimsy affair of paper and the rain had played havoc with it. Philip, who was visited by a sudden feeling of cosiness, watched her turn it over and stare at it with wide grave eyes. Then he saw her shake her head; just like a child, he thought. He wanted to tell her so and give her a quick little hug, a sign across a thousand miles of desert; then rush away to the nearest shelter and talk everything out with her. What was she feeling? How odd it was that he didn't know!

'You look,' she said, holding out the map. 'I can't see anything. It's all a stupid puddle.'

He peered at the thing just to satisfy her. Roads and rivers and stout acres were now so many blotches. 'It seems to me it represents this country very well, for everything here's under water. The thing's useless. Besides I can't make out where we missed the turning.' He followed a possible road with his forefinger, only to discover that it led him into a long blue smudge, under which some fifty square miles were submerged. Perhaps if they went there, everything would be different. Perhaps they were there. 'I give it up,' he told her. Then he turned to see Penderel's tousled hair and bright eyes above the back of the seat. 'Would you like to look at the map, Penderel? We can't make anything of it.'

Penderel grinned and shook his head. 'No map for me. I don't believe we're on a map. Drive on and we'll arrive somewhere. Only don't let it be water. We be land rats.'

Margaret made a slight gesture of impatience. 'It's absurd now trying to get to any particular place. We must stop at the first village we come to and ask for shelter. What's that?' There came a crack of thunder that rolled and clanged among the hills. Philip opened the door on his side, threw away his cigarette, looked out at the thick jigging wires of rain, and then hastily closed the door. 'More rain and thunder,' he said, then looked doubtfully at Margaret. 'We'd better move on and, as you say, get in anywhere.' There arrived with Margaret's nod a savage assent from the sky, another roll and clanging of iron doors on the summits above.

Philip started the engine again. Margaret put out the little observation lamp and with it any fleeting sense of cosiness. The night invaded them once more; they were wet and numbed and maundering on towards a furious autumnal midnight, among cracking mountains, lost in a world of black water; they were sitting crazily behind two lamps that showed nothing but a streaming track, the flashing of the rain, and the gulf beyond. When they moved off, very cautiously hugging the right-hand side, he could hear Penderel's voice raised above the din. He was singing or at least shouting some kind of song, like a man in his bath. The whole night was going to be one vast bath and so Penderel was singing. A queer youth!—Philip looked down on him from a great height, but then suddenly remembered that Penderel was only two years younger than himself. It was his daft drinking and shouting and singing that magnified these two years. Unlike him, Penderel didn't seem to have escaped from the War yet, and every night with him was still the night before one moved up to the line. Why didn't Margaret like him? He wanted to think about Margaret, but just now there wasn't time.

There was another sharp bend in the road, not fifty yards away, and he decided to nose round it very cautiously. What a tremendous rumbling there was! Was it thunder? He shouted to the others. Margaret was leaning forward, peering out. 'Look out, Waverton,' he thought he heard Penderel shout. The bend was here, another corner as sharp as the last, and he pulled round and ran straight into roaring chaos. A torrent of water was pouring down upon the road and something struck the car, a large clod of earth or a rock, with a resounding jolt. The entire slope above seemed to be rumbling and shuttering. In another minute they would be buried or sent flying over the other side of the road. Dazed as he was, he realised that there was just a chance of escape, and he pressed down the accelerator while he kept the other foot trembling on the brake for fear the road in front should be blocked or should have fallen away. So far it seemed to be clear, though the whole hillside immediately behind them now seemed to be crashing down. The road ran back in a curve, probably between two spurs of the hill. Margaret was shrieking in his ear: 'Lights! Look, Phil. Lights! Pull in there.' He saw them not far in front, where the road seemed to bend back again, beyond the centre of its horseshoe curve. Without thinking, he began to slow down. There seemed to be some sort of gateway there, an entrance to a drive perhaps.

Then the rumbling and crashing and tearing behind, growing in volume every moment, awakened him to the danger of the situation.

It was obvious now that there was a house in front, and he could see the open entrance to the drive. But what kind of place was this to stay in, with the whole hillside threatening to descend upon them and tons of water coming down from somewhere? 'We'd better go on while we can,' he shouted to Margaret. 'It's not safe here.' But at the same time he clapped on the brakes and brought the car down to a walking pace. They were now only a few yards from the gateway, were actually sheltered by the high wall of the garden. He felt a vague sense of safety, the sight of that wall keeping at bay the terror of the water and the crumbling slope.

He caught Margaret's 'No, stop!' and instantly obeyed the cry. He did it against his judgment, yet felt partly relieved to be free for a moment from wheels and brakes. She clutched his arm and he could feel her trembling a little. 'Let's stay here,' she was gasping.

'We ought to go on while the road's still open.' His voice was hoarse and he too was shaking.

'Let's get out and see what's happening,' Penderel chimed in. 'I believe the whole damned hill's going. Something's burst up above.' He was opening the door. Horribly cramped, Philip tumbled out and joined him in the black downpour. At least it was good to be on one's legs again, and though the night was hideous, the situation seemed less precarious than it did when one was sitting in there, playing fantastic tricks with mechanism.

'Are we going to push on,' Penderel shouted, 'or stay here and ask these people for shelter? We can't go back, for that road's completely done in. And the road in front may be done in too. I'm for staying here.'

'But listen to that.' The fury behind had not spent itself and even appeared to be gathering force. 'We're close to it,' Philip went on, 'and the whole place seems dangerous to me. It may be all washed away before morning. And really we ought to tell those people what's happening.'

Penderel walked forward, peered through the entrance, and then returned. 'They don't seem to be bothering much about it. Lights on, but no signs of alarm.'

'Perhaps they don't know.' Philip shivered. 'For that matter there may not be anybody there. They may have cleared off.'

Margaret was looking out of the car. 'Why are you standing there?' For once she sounded forlorn. 'I can't stand much more of this. It's a nightmare.'

'Penderel thinks we ought to stay here,' Philip told her. 'But I feel inclined to go on. It isn't safe here and the road in front seems to be still open.' He looked forward as far as he could, and though the road was partly flooded it revealed no dangerous obstacle.

'But is it open?' Penderel asked the question, and Margaret, still peering out, seemed to echo him.

The next moment they were answered. There came a rumble and a following roar, this time in front of them, somewhere not far away in the darkness. It seemed as if a whole side of the hill was slipping or being washed away. The noise was deafening, terrifying, like a great buffeting of the ears; and even the ground beneath their feet seemed to tremble. The road in front had gone, and what was left of the horseshoe bend, the little stretch on which they stood, was now being rapidly flooded. 'Bring her in here,' Penderel shouted, and rushed to the drive, bent on leading the way. Philip hesitated long enough to feel the sudden chill wash of water round his legs, and then clambered back into the car. The rain was streaming down his face and he could hardly see; his hands were so numbed that they were like pieces of wood; but the engine was running and he contrived to jam in the gear and slip the clutch with only the loss of a few seconds. For a moment or two the car roared helplessly, but then it began to move slowly, with a prodigious splashing, and he turned it through the entrance and up the drive, which ran forward at a slight incline. He could see Penderel hurrying in front, a jerky and blurred figure in the rain, just like a man in a film. Now the house, surprisingly large to be in such an out-of-the-way place, towered above them. What was to be done with the car? Philip couldn't decide, so merely turned it round the corner, where the drive curved towards the front door only a few yards away, and then came to a standstill. The head lamps shone upon the house and the door was strongly, dramatically, illuminated by their uncouth glare. It was a large door, stout enough for a little fortress, and three broad steps led up to it. Somehow it looked as if it were closed for ever.

Philip found Penderel looking in at him. 'Benighted!—that's the word,' Penderel said. 'I've been trying to remember it all the way from the gate. I'll go and beg for shelter. What a night! What a place! I like this, though, don't you?'

Philip stared after him as he walked forward to the door. The night was still a tumult, full of a distant rumbling and crashing and the ceaseless drumming of the rain, yet there seemed to fall in it now a sudden quietness. It was the house itself that was so quiet. Driving up like this, you expected a bustle, shadows hurrying across the blinds, curtains lifted, doors flung open. But so far this house hadn't given the slightest sign, in spite of its lighted windows. It seemed strangely turned in upon itself, showing nothing but a blank face in the night. You could hardly imagine that great front door ever being opened at all.

And now Penderel was there at the door, darkening it with his shadow and groping for a knocker. Philip turned to Margaret, who was leaning back, exhausted perhaps. Once inside, out of the night, warmed and dry, eyes meeting eyes again in the light, they could perhaps talk everything out: now was their chance, before they reached home again and custom fell on them like weights of armour. He put out a reassuring hand, and though she didn't meet it with her own, he seemed to catch a faint smile. Did she whisper something? He couldn't tell. All he heard now was Penderel knocking at that door.

CHAPTER II

Penderel thought he would give them another and louder rap. *'Is there anybody there?' said the Traveller.* That's why poetry is so good, he told himself, his hand on the knocker; at such times odd bits of it come shooting up in the mind like rockets. *Rat-tatta-tat-tat.* Should he give them another and conclusive *tat-tat*, rounding off the phrase? No, that always sounded so complete that there was no urgency in it. That was loud enough anyhow, loud enough—as people said in their hellishly grim fashion—to waken the dead. Suppose the people inside *were* dead, all stretched out with the lights quietly burning above them. Suppose one of them was just dying or dead and the others were all crying or praying at the bedside, and he and the Wavertons marched in, 'Can you put us up for the night, please?' But most likely the owner of the house would be a fat little Welsh squire, and the place would be full of dogs and drinks. He could do with the drinks. Everything about him was soaking except his throat, which was Sahara itself. If people are to be sodden, let them be sodden inside, where all the real mischief's done.

There was somebody at the other side of the door at last. He had a feeling that somebody was there, although he couldn't really hear anything. This door, he was positive, would take some opening; you couldn't imagine it flying open; it looked as if somehow it would have to be unscrewed. Yes, something was happening to it. It was creaking. It was moving. Now for it!—a neat little speech.

The door opened an inch or two, and Penderel saw an eye. There was no talking to an eye and so he waited. The eye withdrew and then the door was slowly pulled back. A huge lump of a man stood there, blankly staring at him; a shapeless man with a full black beard and matted hair over a low forehead.

For a minute Penderel himself was all eyes and no tongue, staring blankly back. Then he recovered himself and rapidly plunged into speech.

'We've come to ask for shelter,' he began. 'We got lost and now we're absolutely cut off. We can't go forward or back. The road seems to have gone on each side.'

He broke off for a moment to see if there was any response to his appeal. The man made neither sound nor movement; not a gleam of comprehension lit his face; he just stood there, so much humped flesh and staring eyes. It was as if the door had been opened into Siberia. The thought of the menacing night and the Wavertons waiting there behind him, the contrast between their situation and this senseless immobility suddenly angered him. He raised his voice: 'The road here's under water now. There are floods, landslides. All the mountain side's coming down. We shall have to stay here. Don't you understand?'

If the man did, he gave no sign, but stood there as if he were staring out of another world. Penderel had a sudden desire to pound the great senseless carcase. But then he remembered that they were now in a remote part of Wales, were really travellers in a foreign country, and that it was quite possible that this fellow, who was obviously some kind of servant, could hardly understand English. He might be the solitary surviving specimen of the original aborigines of this island. Penderel knew no Welsh and could only begin all over again, this time raising his voice and introducing some fine descriptive gestures. At the end, the man came to life, though only slowly. First, he lumbered forward a pace, looked towards the car, examined the night, then very laboriously and solemnly shook his head. After that, he tapped Penderel, who looked in silence and amazement as if he were watching the movements of some prehistoric monster, lightly on the chest, pointed indoors, tapped himself on the chest, and ended by producing from somewhere at the back of his throat, a very queer gurgling sound.

This noise made Penderel jump, it was so unexpected. 'What's that?' he cried sharply. Even Welsh ought not to sound like that; it was as if a lump of earth had tried to make a remark.

By way of reply, the man pushed his face near to Penderel's, opened his mouth very wide, and pointed to it with a long dark forefinger. Then he padded away, leaving Penderel to gape through the open door. He must have retired to fetch his master, for it could hardly be his own house, though he looked more like a performing bear than a butler. Penderel wondered whether to walk forward into the large hall visible through the door or to return for a moment to the Wavertons, who must be wondering what was happening. He turned, however, only to find them at his elbow.

'This is absurd,' Mrs. Waverton was declaring indignantly. 'Keeping us here like this! What's the matter?'

He determined to put an easy face upon it.

'The matter has just disappeared, to find somebody, I think. Did you see him? I don't think he's real.'

'What did he say?' Waverton asked.

'Nothing. I don't believe he could say anything. I don't think he knows English or anything else. Wait until you have a good look at him. He's a huge troll who's got all rusty inside.'

Mrs. Waverton, as usual, seemed to brush away this kind of talk. 'Let's go in, Philip. They couldn't refuse to let us stay, an awful night like this. And it's ridiculous standing here.'

'Isn't it?' said Penderel, heartily. 'As if we were carol-singers and this were some kind of devilish Christmas, perhaps Lucifer's birthday.'

'We'll go in then,' said Waverton. 'But what about the car?'

'They'll tell us where to put it later. I must sit down somewhere where there isn't any rain. My head screams with it.' And Mrs. Waverton marched in, followed by the two men.

The first thing that Penderel noticed was that the house had electric light. Somehow he hadn't expected that: it was impossible to imagine the giant troll fingering the switches or going round the accumulators. But the lights weren't behaving properly though; they were jumping and flickering, and they made the whole place jumpy, queerly uncertain. It was the kind of hall you rarely see except on the stage, being both entrance hall and lounge (and, if necessary, dining and drawing rooms), lofty and panelled, with a large open fireplace in the left-hand far corner, a broad staircase running up on the right and a gallery above, with a door immediately on the left and two more on the right. The fire was a smouldering old ruin; the table in the centre was very old; and all the chairs seemed to be faded and crazy. There was something ruinous about the whole place, and though it was gloriously snug after the howling misery of the night outside, it hardly suggested comfort and a warm hospitality. Penderel decided that it had a smell of mice and old newspapers.

They all stood bunched together and dripping near the door, and waited in silence for something to happen. After the first glance round, Penderel fixed his eyes on the staircase, down which—if life were what it ought to be—a lady with a long white train should come sweeping, with a great candlestick in each hand. He watched the stairs jump with the lights, and had a sudden daft desire to rush to the bottom of them, strike an attitude, and say something very romantic at the top of his voice. Enter the three wettest people in Christendom: one of them, obviously a tragic clown, approaches the jumping stairs. What a pity people didn't really think of life as a play, taking care to come on properly, to say and do no more than was necessary, and then to make a good clean exit. If there were any drinks going later, he must point that out to Waverton: it was one of those things you can only say over a drink.

The first door on the right suddenly opened and a thin elderly man in black walked into the hall, halting when he was a few paces from them. He was followed by a waddling old woman who came up and looked them over curiously with eyes like tiny black buttons. At the back was the huge creature, who stood lumpishly near the door.

'My name is Femm,' said the thin man, 'Horace Femm. I cannot understand what is the matter. Our servant, Morgan there, is dumb.' His voice was as thin as he was, very dry and harsh, and he spoke with a curious and disconcerting precision.

Penderel cleared his throat, but Mrs. Waverton cut in before him, hastily giving their names and declaring their errand.

'Shelter?' Mr. Femm looked dubious and put his long hand to his chin. You seemed to hear bone rubbing bone.

'What is it?' the old woman suddenly screamed, making them all jump.

Mr. Femm pushed out his neck, bringing his mouth nearer to the hand she held to her ear. Instead of raising his voice he contrived to make it extraordinarily penetrating by hissing his words. The effect was strangely sinister, and indeed he seemed to turn a malignant eye upon the woman. 'Shelter,' he hissed. 'They want to stay here all night.' It sounded rather like the villain of old-fashioned melodrama.

The other shook her head. 'They can't. We can't have them here.' Although she had examined them so thoroughly, she talked as if they weren't really there.

'You see how it is,' said Mr. Femm, in his ordinary tones. 'My sister, Rebecca here, is somewhat deaf. Morgan, as I have already pointed out, is dumb. My brother, Sir Roderick Femm, the master of this house, is confined to his bed upstairs, very old, very weak, and may not live long. Though not, I beg to assure you, without hospitable instincts, I myself am as rusty as an old file. This house is partly a barn and partly a ruin and could not accommodate you even for a night. I advise you, for your own sakes, to look elsewhere. There is, I believe, an inn about twelve miles from here.'

These people might have been living in another world; they didn't seem to know what was happening all round them; it was time now to make them understand the situation. All three began explaining at once. Mrs. Waverton went up to Miss Femm and shouted in her ear. Penderel and Waverton hustled the uncomprehending Mr. Femm to the open door and confronted him with the black and torrential night itself, through which there still came a menacing roar.

'The road's gone on each side of this house,' cried Waverton, waving a hand to left and right. 'We can't go half a mile, let alone twelve miles. We're cut off from everywhere. Even the road below's under water.'

'For that matter,' Penderel added, determined to show Mr. Femm what sort of world he was living in, 'this place may be under water soon or even buried. The hill's crumbling on each side, and it looks as if something above here, a lake or a reservoir, has burst its banks. Listen to that.' He held up his hand impressively. The roaring really did seem louder than ever. Penderel thought he could hear the distant crashing of rocks.

Mr. Femm retreated a step, his eyes two pin-points in a crumpled sheet of paper. Penderel hadn't seen a man look so frightened for years. What an oddity!—dense at first, and then flying into a panic. A man so thin, with so little flesh and so much shining bone ought to be braver than that; he was almost a skeleton, and skeletons, jangling and defiant, are brave enough. It's our flesh, Penderel told himself, the jellied stuff that rots so easily, which quivers and creeps, goes goosey with fright; but our bones stand up and don't give a damn. This fellow was a fraud.

Mr. Femm had now turned and gone hissing towards his sister. 'Did you hear that?' he asked her. 'They say there's been a landslide on each side of us, and floods too. The lake has burst its banks. We are trapped. We shall have to go. Do you hear?' His voice had almost risen to a scream.

She was now as quiet as he was noisy. She looked him up and down contemptuously, clasped her little fat hands in front of her, and said: 'Yes, I heard. I've expected it after all this rain and rain and rain. It will all come tumbling down again. God is not mocked.' She gloated over this, and looked at her brother triumphantly, her suety face alight with malice. 'You're afraid, Horace. You don't believe in God. Oh, no! But you're afraid to die. You don't believe in His mercy, but now you can believe in His wrath.' She looked at him steadily, and then when he opened his mouth to reply she went on again, more vehemently. 'You've seen His anger in the sky. You've heard Him in the night. And you're afraid. Where's your mocking now?' She stopped, and nobody spoke or stirred for a moment. 'Well, your time hasn't come yet. This house is safe enough. This has happened before, before you came back, Horace, and we were never touched.' She turned her head. 'Morgan, come here,' she shrieked, and when he came towering above her, she screamed up at him: 'You remember the great storm, when we were cut off once before, and there were floods and landslides and the road down there was all washed away? This house was safe then, wasn't it?'

Morgan nodded and made a noise in his beard. Then he made a sweeping gesture to include the whole house, and pointed impressively to the floor.

'Morgan remembers,' cried Miss Femm. 'He means that the house was safe because it stands on a great rock.'

He nodded his head affirmatively again, pointed to the back of the house, raised his finger, and then clenched his fist, grinning trollishly throughout the dumb show.

'He means that this rock comes out at the back of the house and shields it,' Miss Femm explained. 'Morgan remembers the last time we had storms like these, when this was the only place left untouched. And so you see, Horace, we can stay where we are.'

Mr. Femm had now recovered himself. 'It is obvious,' he said, looking at Mrs. Waverton, 'that you will have to remain here for the night. The misfortune is yours, not ours. I am afraid we can promise you very little.'

'No beds,' screamed his sister, with that terrifying unexpectedness of hers. Penderel had begun to cherish an intense dislike of her, and longed to bellow in return, particularly when she gave another screech: 'They can't have beds.'

'As my sister hints,' said Mr. Femm, smoothly, 'there are no beds, I am afraid, at your disposal. Indeed, this is the last house in Britain I should choose to be either a guest or a host in. But please remember that it is not mine.'

'We really don't need beds or anything, thank you. We quite understand,' Mrs. Waverton told him.

'Just a roof,' added Waverton.

'And a fire,' Penderel put in. And for the love of Mike, he whispered to himself, a drink too. A brief tussle with floods and landslides was sufficiently heartening in itself, but an acquaintance with this house, these people, was not to be undertaken feeling all cold and dark inside, without a drink.

A faint suggestion of geniality, like a leaden and watery gleam of November sunshine, crept into Mr. Femm's manner. 'Of course, of course! We can offer you a roof and a fire and some food and drink. You can spend the night sitting round the fire here, perhaps the best place a night like this. I am not sure that I want to go to bed myself to-night. Morgan, attend to the fire. You must make yourselves as comfortable as you can.' He bent forward again and hissed: 'Perhaps we could have supper soon, Rebecca.'

'I'll see that they have some supper, Horace,' cried his sister. 'Don't give yourself airs. You're not the master here.'

'What about the car?' Waverton asked. 'Is there anywhere I could put it where it would be safe all night?'

'Your motor car? You have it outside there?' Mr. Femm twisted his long dry fingers and called Morgan from the fire. 'There are out-houses, round the corner there, on the left, where we only keep a horse and a trap now. There might be room for a motor car there. Morgan will know. Morgan, go with this gentleman and see if there is room for his motor car in the stables or coach-house.' Morgan nodded sullenly and lurched towards the door.

'What about the bags?' Waverton looked at both his wife and Penderel.

'We'll get them in,' Penderel replied.

Mrs. Waverton was emphatic. 'I simply must have mine,

Philip. I'm soaked to the skin and must change my things. Bring the bags in now.'

Darkness and rain and a vague tumult still held the night. 'Thank God I'm now seeing the last of this car to-night,' Waverton said, as they tugged at the straps round the luggage grid. 'We're well out of this, though I must say this is a queer house.'

'A very queer house and very queer people,' Penderel replied, pulling at the swollen leather. 'I now know the real meaning of the phrase, "Cherchez les Femms." I've taken this old bag of mine into some damned odd places, but I have a feeling this is going to be about the oddest.'

Waverton grunted. 'It's better than capering in the dark along roads that aren't there, anyhow. It's safe and there's a roof and a fire.'

'Nothing's safe,' said Penderel, swinging out two bags. 'Perhaps this is the fire, and we're merely taking the bags out of the frying-pan.' He hurried round to the door and did not hesitate to jostle Morgan, who had been standing in the doorway all the time. If the man didn't like it, he could lump it, and lumping it seemed to be all he could do. A gorilla would have been a little more amiable and helpful: the man overdid his dumbness and his part as giant troll.

They all began bustling about now, just as if the hall had been suddenly turned into a railway station, Penderel thought. Mrs. Waverton, looking less like a superior person than usual (she was really rather pretty), shed her sodden hat and coat, pounced upon one of the bags, and was now exchanging confidential little shrieks with Miss Femm. Waverton had gone out again, accompanied by Morgan, and was now steering his car round the corner into the coach-house or shed or whatever it was. Mr. Femm had gone creaking away somewhere. Penderel did his best to join in the bustle, but when he had taken off his heavy dripping coat and had flung it over his bag near the door, there was nothing left for him to do. He lit a cigarette, sat down near the fire, and dreamily regarded his steaming outstretched legs and enjoyed the creeping warmth. He was tired. Images of his companions came floating by like spectral ships: Mrs. Waverton, one of those pale and clear and terrifically educated women who knew everything and who knew nothing, never actually breaking through into the real world; Philip Waverton himself, crammed with shy sense and honest-to-God feeling, but too anxious, too married, too well broken-in; the Femms here, the string-and-bone dithering male and the fat and somehow obscene female, with her revivalist God, and that tongueless hulk of a Morgan. And there was another somewhere, upstairs in bed. What was his name? Sir Roderick—that was it. Old Sir Roderick, the master of the house, doomed to be for ever upstairs silent and unseen. Did he ever give any orders? Perhaps Rebecca brought them down—what was it?—written on tables of stone.

The next moment Penderel could have groaned aloud. Suddenly that old feeling had returned. It came, as usual, without warning. A grey tide, engulfing all colour and shape of things that had been or were to be, rushed across his mind, sweeping the life out of everything and leaving him all hollow inside. Once again he sat benumbed in a shadow show. Yet as ever—and this was the cruel stroke—there was something left, left to see that all the lights were being quenched, left to cry out with a tiny crazed voice in the grey wastes. This was what mattered, this was the worst, and black nights and storms and floods and crumbling hills were not to be compared with this treachery from within. It wasn't panic nor despair, he told himself, that made so many fellows commit suicide; it was this recurring mood, draining the colour out of life and stuffing one's mouth with ashes. One crashing bullet and there wasn't even anything left to remember what had come and gone, to cry in the mind's dark hollow; life could then cheat as it liked, for it did not matter; you had won the last poor trick.

Having conjured the malady into a phrase or two, Penderel felt better, came out of his reverie and looked about for entertainment. He found it in the person of Mr. Femm, who was bearing down upon him, carrying a small tray. There was a bottle on the tray, and Penderel felt like breaking into applause. Flourish of trumpets: enter Bottle.

'Now do you think, Mr.—er——' Mr. Femm put down the tray and hesitated.

'Penderel,' he told him promptly—told the bottle too.

'Mr. Penderel, of course,' said Mr. Femm. 'Do you think you could join me in a drink?'

'Mr. Femm, I feel that I could, with pleasure, join you in a drink.' They were like two old club cronies.

Mr. Femm stood over the bottle. 'It is not whisky, which all you young men drink now, I believe. This is gin, which I prefer to all the other spirits, except, of course, the very old brandies. With some lemon, a little sugar perhaps, some hot water if you care for it, gin is excellent, and, remember, the purest of the spirits.'

'I do remember,' said Penderel, heartily. 'Gin for me, with pleasure. I used to drink it with the sea-dogs. The Navy, at least the commissioned part of it, has a passion for gin. After it gave up rum, it went straight to gin. The brave fellows sit round all night, dropping remarks about turbines and torpedoes, the coast of Manchuria, and beautiful blue-eyed girls, and drinking gin with admirable steadiness and ease.' He watched the other pour out the liquor, accepted lemon and sugar, refused water, and then, glass in hand, remarked: 'We must have a toast.'

Mr. Femm looked thoughtful, even philosophic, with the faint ghost of conviviality hovering about him. 'Mr. Penderel, I give you a toast that you will not appreciate, being young. I give you—Illusion!' And he lifted his glass.

'I'm all for it. Illusion!' He gasped a little for it was unusually strong stuff. But that was better. A few more such toasts and illusion would be something more than a wistful sentiment. 'But don't imagine that I'm too young to appreciate the value of illusion. I'm just the right age. I was born too late or too early to escape the rotten truth, and I've been stubbing my toes against flinty facts ever since I left school.'

Mr. Femm smiled grimly. He was about to say that that itself was one of youth's illusions. Penderel could see it coming: he had heard it before. But then Mr. Femm surprised him by not speaking at all; he merely stared on after the smile had vanished and took a sip from his glass. The next moment his eyes seemed to be looking out into horrible space, and his face was twitching. He appeared to be listening. 'A dreadful night,' he muttered at last. 'It seems to be getting worse.'

'It's a brute, certainly,' Penderel replied, 'but apparently there's no danger here. Miss Femm and your man seem to be positive that this house is safe enough.'

'But even if it is, we may be completely cut off, shut in here.' The man seemed to be talking to himself rather than to Penderel.

'We might, of course, and that would be a nuisance for you.' Penderel tried to look polite and anxious and sorry, though he did not care a fig if he had to stay there. He was as well off there as anywhere else. He had nowhere to go, nowhere he even wanted to go, now. Good God!—what a thing to admit to oneself at twenty-nine! 'What I mean is,' he went on, 'that it's a nuisance your having us here like this, besieged with you.'

Mr. Femm looked at him with real terror in his face. There was no mistaking it now. He lashed himself into a kind of anger as frightened men frequently do. 'But to go running out there,' and he pointed shakily at the door, still open to the night, 'in the dark, with the floods there, the rocks tumbling down, everything cold and black and pitiless. And nowhere else to go, no escape!' And he clashed together his bony hands.

Penderel stared at him. 'A bad business, certainly, if one had to go. But one hasn't, you know. Even if we have to go, you won't have to. You can stay comfortably here.' And as he said this, he looked Mr. Femm in the eyes.

Mr. Femm met the look for a second and then quickly glanced round the room. He was obviously taking hold of himself. Finally he leaned forward. 'As you can probably see,' he whispered, 'I am nervous at the thought of our being shut in here. The fact is that Morgan, who is an old servant of my brother's, is an uncivilised brute. Occasionally he drinks heavily—a night like this would set him going—and once he is drunk he is very dangerous. He is as strong as an ox and could batter a door in with ease. You can imagine that I dread being compelled to remain here, with no means of escape, with such a savage.'

Penderel nodded reassuringly. 'We must try to keep the drink away from him. As a drunk and disorderly, he'd be no joke.' But he had been observing Mr. Femm very narrowly throughout his speech. All this about Morgan might be true, it probably was true, for obviously the man was almost a savage, but nevertheless Penderel was convinced that his companion was lying. It wasn't the thought of Morgan that had terrified him. There was something else; some more fearful image had haunted him when he had so suddenly and strangely cried out against remaining in the house. Perhaps there was something here even worse than a drunk and half-crazed Morgan battering doors in. Perhaps too it was only some maggot of the brain. These Femms, perched remotely on their hill, seemed to have gone queer, all maggot-brained. For a moment he stared at the one before him as if he were staring at a creature from an unknown continent.

The door behind them closed. Morgan was bolting it, and Waverton, doffing his coat, was at their elbow. 'I've put the car away,' he told Penderel. 'Just round the corner in a kind of open shed. It seems safe enough there.' He glanced round. 'Where's my wife?'

Penderel jerked a thumb to the far door on the right. 'Gone to change, I think.' Mr. Femm, still looking somewhat shaken, rose and indicated the bottle and glasses. 'Have some gin, Waverton?' Penderel suggested. 'It's jolly good.'

Waverton smiled and shook his head. 'No, thanks. I don't like the stuff. Are you drinking it, Penderel? Neat, too? It'll make you feel desperately melancholy.'

'Gin is saddening,' Penderel admitted, 'but it's not so

saddening as no gin.' Mr. Femm began to fill the glasses again. His hand was still trembling, and he seemed as jumpy as the daft lights, though indeed these were so bad now that they made everything seem jumpy. Such lights were crazier than darkness itself; they were like a man doing a witch-doctor's dance in a top hat and frock coat. Penderel noticed that Waverton, now no longer a manipulator of brakes and gears but a human being, was looking about him curiously and stealing an odd glance or two at friend Femm. And well he might, Penderel told himself, and suddenly felt unreasonably sorry for Waverton. Somehow he felt that Waverton ought not to be there. Waverton wasn't like him, a man without a load, almost outlawed, naked, but a fellow who had given— what was it?—yes, hostages to fortune. He had, for example, a wife there, now changing her clothes. How odd women were, always either not quite human or too human! She had gone off to change, accompanied by a little fat deaf monster. There was something curiously pathetic about this going off and changing. In a minute she would come tripping back, all dressed up and smiling, just as if it were a party, perhaps somebody's birthday. Penderel had an odd impulse to shake Waverton by the hand, but he restrained it and stretched out his hand for the glass instead. He must, though, talk to Waverton about Mr. Femm.

CHAPTER III

Margaret felt relieved at the very sight of her bag. Five minutes with it in private and she would be herself again. Dry clothes and a comb through her hair would settle everything. The last ten minutes had been dreadful. She felt all wet round her shoulders and knees, and so bedraggled, so effaced by rain and rushing darkness, that she could hardly think of herself as having the outward appearance of a complete real person. It was like being a tattered ghost; you couldn't possibly face anything. It had been worse coming in here, meeting these people, than it was in the actual danger outside. The moment you were less than yourself, people were the worst of all. There had been one awful second, when this queer creature, Miss Femm, had been screaming at her brother, when she had suddenly wanted to scream herself, to clutch at Philip, to drag him to the door, back to the car. It was absurd. But she was wet and tired; the storm had got on her nerves. Once neat outside, cosy within, she would be ready to face anything. Now for some dry things at last.

She picked up her bag and walked up to Miss Femm. 'I'm dreadfully wet,' she said, producing a splendid woman-to-woman smile. 'May I go and change my things?'

'What?' the woman screamed at her. Of course, she was deaf. How annoying deaf people were, and how queer: they seemed scarcely human. Margaret repeated her request in a loud voice, but this time without the smile. She felt like a ridiculous little girl.

Miss Femm nodded. 'You look wet. You go and change your clothes.'

'A bathroom perhaps?' Margaret shouted. How silly she sounded! 'Will you please show me where to go?'

'You'll have to go in my bedroom. That's all there is.'

There was no note of apology in this. Miss Femm seemed to be enjoying herself. 'There's no bathroom, not now. It's all in ruins. You couldn't get inside the door. We're all in ruins here. You'll have to put up with it.' Only the tiny snapping eyes were alive in that doughy face of hers. They went travelling over Margaret like two angry little exiles in a hateful country.

'I quite understand. It's very good of you to have us here.' Margaret made a movement to show that she was tired of standing there with the bag in her hand.

'Come with me then.' Miss Femm turned and went waddling away. Margaret, following behind, expected her to make for the staircase and was surprised to find her going towards a door on the left. They passed through this door and walked down a very dimly lit corridor that had an uncarpeted stone floor. Margaret shivered: the place was like a cellar. There was a big window on the left, without curtains, brightly slashed with rain until she came up to it, and then it was all black, with the night roaring outside. This must be the back of the house then. A little further on, however, they came to a door on the same side as the window. Miss Femm halted, her hand on the knob. It flashed upon Margaret that if this door were opened the wind and the rain and the darkness would come in, and they would walk through it back into the night. But she must be sensible; this wasn't the place for silly fancies; there must be a little wing, of course, jutting out here.

'You came yourselves, didn't you?' cried Miss Femm, still standing at the door. 'You thought it better to be here than out there, eh? Well, you'll have to put up with it. We're all going to pieces here. You'd have been proud to come here once; you'd have thought my brother, Sir Roderick, a great man then; and so he was, in a way. But not in God's way. None of them were that. And now they're all rotting, going to pieces, choked with dust, like this house. We've done with life here, what you'd call life.' Her voice had risen to a scream again.

There was no reply to this and Margaret didn't try to make any. With someone else she might have ventured some soothing meaningless remark, but you couldn't do that at the top of your voice. The woman was obviously a little mad, probably touched with religious mania, and if she had lived here all her life there was some excuse for her. After all, there was no reason to be alarmed. These were only the old apologies (I'm afraid you'll find us all upset, Mrs. Waverton) in a new fantastic shape. So she said nothing, but nodded sympathetically. There was something comforting in the very weight of the bag she was holding.

Miss Femm opened the door. 'I've none of this electric light. I won't have it. You'll have to wait till I've lit the candles.' She went in and Margaret waited in the doorway. The room was not quite dark for a sullen glow of firelight crept about in it. Margaret took heart. A fire was more than she had expected. It was all going to be quite pleasant. Two candles were alight now, one on a rather high mantelshelf and the other on a little dressing-table. 'Come in,' Miss Femm shouted, 'and shut the door.'

The room was not very large; it seemed to be crowded with heavy furniture; and it was closely shuttered. You couldn't imagine it ever having had an open window. The place was muggy and stale, smelling as if it were buried deep in dirty old blankets. On the left was a big bed, piled suffocatingly high with clothes, and an enormous wardrobe so top-heavy that it seemed to be falling forward. A wood fire smouldered in a little iron grate. On the other side of the fireplace were a massive chest of drawers, looking as if they bulged with folded alpaca and flannel and moth-balls, the little dressing-table, which had a tiny cracked mirror on it, and a dismal wash-hand stand. The walls seemed to be crowded with old-fashioned oleographs and steel engravings of an hysterically religious kind, full of downy-bearded and ringleted Saviours, and with ornamented texts about the Prince of Love and the Blood of the Lamb. Having once glanced round, Margaret kept her eyes away from the walls. Next week, to-morrow even, these things would probably seem funny; the whole room would be a remembered joke; but at the moment it was all rather horrible. It was all so thick and woolly and smelly.

There was a chair near the fire and Margaret promptly took possession of it. She felt rather sick. Miss Femm, a thick little image, stood watching her at the other side of the fireplace. Why didn't the creature go? Margaret pulled the bag towards her and began to unfasten it. 'Thank you,' she called, looking up. 'I can manage quite well now.' It was a relief to see her own things, so familiar, so sensible, snugly waiting her in the open bag.

Miss Femm suddenly shattered the silence. 'I stay down here,' she shrieked, 'because it's less trouble and it's quiet. My sister Rachel had this room once, after she'd hurt her spine. She died here. I was only young then, but she was younger than I was, only twenty-two when she died. That was in ninety-three—before you were born, eh?'

Margaret nodded and kicked off a shoe. She hoped this wasn't opening a chapter of reminiscence. She wanted to change and get out of this place. The very thought of the hall, with Philip and the others there, seemed pleasant now.

'Rachel was a handsome girl, wild as a hawk, always laughing and singing, tearing up and down the hills, going out riding. She was the great favourite. My father and Roderick worshipped her and let her have all her own way. All the young men that came followed her about. Then it was all Rachel, Rachel, with her big brown eyes and her red cheeks and her white neck. She found a young man to please her at last, but one day she went out riding and they brought her back in here. She was six months on that bed, and many an hour I spent listening to her screaming. I'd sit there by the bedside and she'd cry out for me to kill her, and I'd tell her to turn to Jesus. But she didn't, even at the end. She was godless to the last.'

With both shoes off now, Margaret was waiting impatiently for the woman to go. She didn't want to listen, but there was no escape from that screeching voice nor from the image it called up of the long-dead Rachel Femm, who would remain with her like a figure from a bad dream. Somehow she felt as if the broad road of life were rapidly narrowing to a glittering wire. She must hurry, hurry. She stood up, pointedly turned her back on her companion, and began taking things out of the bag.

But Miss Femm did not stir. In another minute she was talking again, this time, it would seem, more to herself than to Margaret. 'They were bad enough before here, but after Rachel died they were worse. There was no end to their mocking and blaspheming and evil ways. They were all accursed, whether they stayed here or went away. I see that now. They were all branded. They were marked down one by one. I see His hand in it now. And it's not finished yet. Sometimes He will reveal his great plan to the least of His servants. He's out there to-night. He's out there now.'

This was awful. In despair, Margaret sat down and began peeling off her stockings. She knew that the woman's eyes were now fixed upon her; she could feel their beady stare.

Miss Femm was quieter now that her interest had narrowed to Margaret. 'You're married, aren't you?'

Margaret reached out for her towel so that she could dry her feet. 'Yes. My husband's out there in the hall.' Philip turned into something different, something intangible and yet substantial, like a big account in a bank, as soon as she called him my husband. This thing was not to be confused with the exciting personal adventure called Philip.

'Which one?' Miss Femm was asking. 'The quiet dark one or the other?'

'Yes, the quiet dark one.' Margaret rubbed away and suddenly felt proud of Philip for being a quiet dark one.

'The other's a godless lad. I saw him. There isn't much I don't see. He's got wild eyes, and he's one of Satan's own. I've seen too many of them, coming here laughing and singing and drinking and bringing their lustful red and white women here, not to know. He'll come to a quick bad end. If I'd have known, he wouldn't have set foot in this house.' Miss Femm was screaming again and she had now moved forward a pace or two. But it was quite evident that she had no intention of going, so Margaret did not hesitate any longer but continued changing hastily. The room was horribly oppressive; you seemed to breathe dirty old wool. As she pulled on dry stockings she was annoyed to find that her hands were trembling.

'Yes, they'd even bring their women here.' Miss Femm's voice was edged with hate. 'This house was filled with sin. Nobody took any notice of me, except to laugh. Even the women, brazen lolling creatures, smothered in silks and scents, would laugh. They went years ago, and they're not laughing now, wherever they are. And you don't hear any laughing here. If I came among them—my own father and brothers, my own blood—they'd tell me to go away and pray, though they never used to tell Rachel to go away and pray. Yes, and I went away and prayed. Oh yes, I prayed.'

This was poor crazed stuff, but Margaret seemed to hear those prayers, terribly freighted. She stood up now, before pulling off her dress, and saw, so vividly in the candle-light from the mantelshelf, one side of the swollen face, a fungus cheek. It looked like grey seamed fat, sagging into putrefaction. The woman's whole figure seemed so much dead matter, something that would just stay there and rot. Only her voice and her little eyes were alive, but these were dreadfully alive; and they would remain, screeching and cursing, staring and snapping, when everything else had rotted. Oh, what nonsense was this? The poor old creature was infecting her. She must be sensible, she told herself, and found relief in pulling off her dress.

After the last outburst, Miss Femm's mood seemed to change. 'I've kept myself free from all earthly love, which is nothing but vanity and lusts of the flesh. You'll come to see that in time, and then it may be too late to give yourself, as I've done, to the Lord. Just now, you're young and handsome and silly, and probably think of nothing but your long straight legs and white shoulders and what silks to put on and how to please your man; you're revelling in the joys of fleshly love, eh?'

Margaret was only too glad that she was busy rubbing her

shoulders with the towel, for this talk made her want to rub and rub, to wipe every word away as soon as it reached her. This stuff was even worse than the other. She towelled away at her bared arms and shoulders and made no reply.

Miss Femm didn't seem to care. She went on staring, and said at last: 'Have you given him a child?'

That, at least, could be answered. 'Yes, we've one child,' Margaret told her, 'a girl, four years old. Her name's Betty.' How queer to think of Betty now! She suddenly saw her asleep in that nursery, far away, not merely in Hampstead, in another world. But no, Betty wasn't in another world—that was the awful thing—she had come into the same world as this Femm woman, yes, and that other, Rachel, who had once screamed on that bed. Her heart shook. She wanted to rush back to Betty at once.

'Betty,' Miss Femm began. 'I once knew a Betty.'

'I don't want to hear, I don't want to hear,' Margaret repeated to herself, and somehow contrived to beat off the words that followed as she picked up the blue dress she had taken out of her bag. It was a lovely dress—almost new, and Philip and Muriel Ainsley had both admired it—and it might conquer everything, make this night all clean and sensible again at a stroke. Lovingly she unfolded it.

When she looked up again, she was surprised to find that Miss Femm, now silent, was much nearer than she had been before. The eyes in that swollen, grey, fatty mask were now fixed upon her. She shivered, suddenly feeling as if she were standing there naked.

Miss Femm came nearer, stretched out a hand and touched the dress. 'That's fine stuff, but it'll rot. And that's finer stuff still, but it'll rot too in time.'

'What's finer stuff?' Margaret was looking down at her dress as she asked the question.

'That is.' And the hand that had been fingering the dress was suddenly pushed flatly and coldly against the bare skin, just above her right breast.

Margaret sprang back, sick and dazed, all her skin shuddering from that toad-like touch. 'Don't!' she gasped. She was going to fall, to faint; the room was slithery with beastliness, dark with swarming terrors. Then anger came shooting up like a rocket, and cleared the air. She felt herself towering. 'How dare you!' she blazed at her. She made a sudden movement, shaking herself, and Miss Femm retreated, mumbling.

There was a knock at the door. Margaret jumped and looked round, then turned to Miss Femm, who was still mumbling. 'There's someone at the door,' she shouted. 'You'd better see who it is.' The other looked across, and then, without a word, took the candle from the mantelshelf and went slowly to the door, opened it an inch or two and peeped out. The next moment it had shut behind her.

The room darkened and grew as soon as Miss Femm had left it. But of course there was only one candle now; it sent Margaret's shadow sprawling gigantically across the foot of the bed. She turned her eyes away. She did not want to look at that bed. It was growing ghostly; the whole room was filling with ghosts. If she looked at that bed long enough she might see a wasted hand thrust out of it, and meet the eyes of that girl, Rachel Femm. She had heard Rebecca Femm, perhaps it was time now for her to hear Rachel Femm. No, no; things were not really like that; they kept their sanity even if people didn't; it was only yourself that pushed you over the edge, where the horrors began. She wouldn't look again, but she'd be sensible inside and busy herself with the familiar comforting things.

But she couldn't put on that dress yet: she didn't feel clean; she wouldn't feel really clean for days, but something could be done to wipe away that hand. She could feel it yet. There was some water in a jug on the wash-hand stand. She stared at it for a moment, disliking the thought of using it, but finally dipped her towel in it and then rubbed herself hard. She was very tired now and still trembling a little, but the rubbing made her feel better. After she had put on her dress she sat down in front

of the little cracked mirror (turning a twitching back to the
ghosts) and hastily, shakily, tidied her hair. The familiar reflection brought comfort to her; its peeping blue eyes and lifted
mouth sent a message to say that she was Margaret Waverton,
that Philip was waiting for her a few yards away, that the car
was only round the corner, that they were merely taking
shelter in a funny old house among the Welsh mountains.
After that message she had time to powder her nose. Then
she put away all the things she had taken off and fastened the
bag. I'm treating you now, she told the house, as if you were
a railway station; you're not worthy of having an open bag in
you and some stockings left to dry.

She could go now, walk out of this horrible room for ever.
(How did she know she could? What if she were brought back
in here, to lie in that bed and scream, like Rachel Femm?)
She took up the candle and her eye fell on a text just above:
The Lord is my Shepherd. She suddenly saw a vast herd of
Rebecca Femms. What was their shepherd like? And somewhere behind all that was a beautiful idea, something to do
with Betty snuggled into her pillow or with Philip smoking
his pipe in the garden on summer nights; and it was all buried,
suffocated. The very air of this room, atmosphere made out
of dirty wool, would suffocate anything. Well, it was her turn
now: she would show this room something, however badly
she might be behaving. So she put down her candle, drew back
the heavy curtains from the window, jerked up the blind, and,
after a struggle with the rusty fastenings and the stiff cord,
opened the window. The night came roaring in with a sweep
of wind and rain, but the air was unbelievably fresh and sweet.
She stood there for a moment, lifting her face towards the now
friendly darkness, and strangely she felt the tears gathering
in her eyes. A gust of wind blew out the candle. She turned
away, found her bag, and walked to the door. When she came
to close it from outside she could see nothing of the room, for
now all was darkness there, but she seemed to hear the rain,
blown in through the window, faintly pattering on the floor.

As she went back along the corridor she decided that she wouldn't tell Philip what had happened. She wanted to tell him, but that would have to wait; she couldn't tell him until things were absolutely dead right between them again, when they would begin once more to share everything, halving thoughts and swapping dreams. Things ought to be like that now, this very minute, she told herself; it would make all the difference here, in this place, where one was so lonely, lost. If she had known this was going to happen—but then of course she hadn't. She never thought of things like this, and Philip did—it had been one of her complaints, that silly anxiousness of his—and he ought to have made the move. They could have walked into this together then, just a dark night's adventure. She had had an impulse to say something too, earlier, but you couldn't break the months of smooth politeness (Did you sleep well? Very well, thanks. Did you?) with a few words shouted in a car during an incessant downpour. And now she couldn't begin. It would be nothing but humiliating surrender, with Philip pretending elaborately to her that it wasn't. No, this night at least she must see it through in silence.

She had probably seen the worst of it, though, and everything would now become sensible again instead of getting more and more out of hand, opening pits under your feet. (Though nerves accounted for most of it; and days and nights of rain and Penderel's company—he loved to make the simplest thing seem sinister and unmanageable, even his stupid jokes were wild, unpleasant—would account for nerves.) The rest would be merely discomfort and the writhing memory of that room. But if there were only another woman there (not that horror), someone of her own kind who would understand a word or a glance, it would be better.

Yes, everything was all right, she told herself as she pushed open the door into the hall. The men were there, looking comfortable enough. And there were signs of supper on the table. Food—even if that woman had a hand in it—would make a difference. She walked across to them, smiling. Would they notice that something had happened to her? Philip might, and he was looking at her, smiling too, though rather vaguely. Now that she saw him again, that room seemed miles away, shrank to a pin-point of terror.

She put down the bag and walked up to Philip. 'You must have wondered what had become of me,' she told him.

'No, they told me you'd gone to change.' He was surprisingly casual.

'Didn't you think I'd been a long time?' she asked, hoping that he wouldn't think she was fishing for a compliment as she used to do in the old days.

He shook his head and smiled. 'I didn't expect you back so soon. You've been quicker than usual.'

It was astonishing. She felt as if she had been away for hours, just because she had gone through that adventure, been jammed into all manner of queer horrible lives for a few minutes, while they had smoked a cigarette or two and chatted by the fire. 'I seem to have been away a long time,' she replied lamely. It was rather frightening, this difference in the point of view, leaving you so lonely.

'Good for you, Mrs. Waverton!' Penderel called out to her from the other side of the fireplace. 'You make it look like a party. I knew you would. And there's supper coming, though of course it's not polite to mention it.'

It was one of his silly remarks, but for once he did not irritate her and she smiled across at him. But, strangely enough, instead of giving her his usual grin in return, he gave her a curiously unsmiling but kind, even sympathetic, glance. It was just as if he knew what had been happening. That, of course, was absurd, but still there was something very strange in his look.

'Supper will be ready in a few minutes, Mrs. Waverton,' said a harsh voice at her elbow. This was that long bony creature, Mr. Femm. She had forgotten his existence, but now she looked at him with a new and rather creepy interest. 'We have very little to offer you, I am afraid,' he went on, 'but you will understand that we were not expecting company. We have to live very simply here.' He moved forward to help Morgan, who had just entered, to unload a tray. Morgan too she had almost forgotten, and now she looked curiously at his bearded sullen face and gigantic bulk. For one moment he raised his heavy head and his eyes met hers and some kind of intelligence seemed to dawn in them. Then, from behind him, a third figure appeared, to busy itself at the table. It was Miss Femm.

Philip was asking her if she was hungry. 'I am; just about ready for anything,' he added. 'And by the way, we're probably entirely cut off by this time. It's just possible, I understand, that soon we couldn't get out of the house even if we wanted to do. Not that it matters, of course, for a few hours, an odd night. We're not too badly off here, though probably there won't be much sleep for us.' It was just the kind of thing she had wanted to avoid doing, but somehow it was done before she could think. She had slipped a hand through his arm and was now pressing it close.

CHAPTER IV

Penderel left his chair, and the three of them, making a little group in front of the fire, talked in whispers. Margaret had released Philip's arm and was now feeling rather foolish. She had just caught sight of a loaf of bread and a large piece of cheese, and the solid ordinariness of them had suggested to her that she was in danger of behaving like a tired hysterical woman.

'It's absurd,' said Penderel, 'that we should have to be so secretive about food. Why should we have to pretend it isn't there until our hosts point it out to us? I'd like to live in a country where all guests gathered round the table and were expected to make comments as each dish appeared. They'd say: "What's this you're putting on the table? Oh, yes, splendid! We all like that"; or "Don't bring that cabbage in for us. We never touch it." What do you think?'

'It would suit me,' said Philip. 'But I don't know how hostesses would like it.'

'They wouldn't,' Margaret replied for them. 'It would be beastly.' She liked the glance that Philip had given her; it wasn't so blank; there was friendliness, a hint of long intimacy, in it. She smiled at him.

Philip returned the smile. 'You don't understand hostesses, Penderel. I suspect you've never really been behind the scenes.' But his thoughts were with Margaret. She was different somehow. She was thawing. He wished there was time and opportunity to talk, really to talk, with all cards quietly set out on the table. Perhaps there would be, later. This would be just the place for it, so remote, so strange, where, so to speak, you couldn't hide any cards as you could at home.

Penderel thought he would keep on, though really he had nothing to say. He was like a hostess himself. But they seemed to like it, and it eased the situation. 'Now that's not true,' he cried. 'I have imagination, and we imaginative fellows are always behind the scenes, and so we suffer with all our hosts and hostesses but must only smile and smile, like true guests. Women don't suffer like that, do they, Mrs. Waverton, because though they know what's going on when they are guests, they don't identify themselves with it, but stand on their dignity as guests and are as aloof as High Court judges.'

'No, they don't, Mr. Penderel.' She was sharp but very friendly. She liked him much better here than she had done in the outside world, in civilisation. 'They only appear to do. It's no use: you can't deceive us. You don't understand women at all. You don't know anything about them.'

'That's true,' Penderel confessed. 'I don't understand 'em. I don't even pretend to. Another thing, I don't like the fellows who do.'

'Neither do I,' said Philip. 'It's a funny thing, but the men who write little books about women, or lecture about them, or pretend to specialise in them in their novels are always complete bounders. You must have noticed that, Penderel?' He had said this before—he could almost read the number of times in Margaret's glance, demure, amused, tolerant—but he spoke with conviction. The thought of those greasy experts suddenly annoyed him.

'I have noticed it.' Penderel was very emphatic. 'They're nasty, crawly lads, who'd be better employed selling lipsticks. Why women themselves can't see it, I don't know. They seem to love 'em.'

'There you go again!' Margaret was amused by the pair of them, so intolerant and self-righteous, so young mannish. 'I believe the secret of your hostility is simple jealousy. You're both jealous because these men seem to be so attractive.' They instantly denied the charge, but let her continue. 'And anyhow, sensible women don't like them very much, probably don't like them at all in their heart of hearts. But one can't help being interested and curious, of course.'

'One can,' said Philip, gloomily, 'or one ought to try. Too many people are interested and curious nowadays. We're all becoming tasters. We sit at the back of our minds watching our sensations like people at a music hall, and we find ourselves yawning between the turns. It's impossible to be happy, or even cheerful, that way. I'm no better than anybody else; we seem to be all alike. But I do draw the line somewhere. If some silly bounder of a woman became a Man expert, and wrote little books or went round lecturing on Man, I wouldn't waste a minute reading her or go a yard to hear her talk. Very few men would.'

'No, and simply because you are all so conceited,' Margaret told him. She was beginning to enjoy this, and for the moment had even forgotten where they were. 'We're so anxious to have men's opinion because we're not conceited, though, thank goodness, we're beginning to lose our silly humility. You are convinced that no woman could tell you anything worth hearing about yourselves; but even if you thought she could, you'd still take care to keep out of the way so that your complacency shouldn't be disturbed.'

'There's something in that,' Philip admitted, and immediately thought how complacent he sounded. Was he really? Margaret was waking up delightfully, suddenly flowering in this darkness.

Penderel was staring about him. 'I suppose this counts as dining-out. In a day or two we shall be able to say: "The other night when I dined with the Femms." That brings it down to commonplace, lets the daylight in, with a crash. I don't know why it should, but it does.'

'I'm glad it does,' said Philip. 'I like the commonplace. It's the little trim lighted bit of life, with God-knows-what waiting for you if you just go over the edge. Some people I know say they hate waking in the morning and leaving their dreams, but it seems to me that either they must lead a ghastly waking life or they must be crazy. I'm always glad to wake in the morning and find myself out of my dreams, which always turn me into a poor shaking barbarian wandering in the dark, compelled to do some idiotic thing with terror all round me. Ordinary life's bad enough, but it's a prince to the stuff we spin out of our rotten unconsciousnesses every night. Don't you think so?'

'I'm not sure.' Penderel stopped to consider the question. 'I think I must be one of the other people. I often have a splendid time in dreams, and hate waking up. Perhaps when I wake up, I land into one of your dreams. It sounds like it from your description of them, which seems to me a fair account of life on some days. Perhaps we're all mixed up, your dreams are my waking life, and so on.'

'Just like Alice, in "Through the Looking Glass," you know,' said Margaret. 'She was told she was only part of the King's dreams—was it the Red King or the White one?—and didn't she begin to cry? I remember how I used to be awfully sorry for her.'

'Yes. Supposing that Mr. Femm there was dreaming us!' And then Penderel was sorry he had spoken. He thought Mrs. Waverton looked startled, as if she had suddenly remembered something that had been forgotten during their prattle. But what could she have remembered? Simply that they were here. Or had she learned something while she was out of the room with the queer Miss Femm? Perhaps she knew what he did not know, namely, why Mr. Femm was so frightened. How strange if she were harbouring, behind that bright face, some fearful piece of knowledge, the image of some terrifying shape!

'More likely that we're dreaming them.' Philip lowered his voice. 'Not Femm himself perhaps, though he's queer enough. But the other two. They're just the kind of people I might dream about, particularly that great dumb fellow— what's his name?—Morgan. He's the worst.'

Margaret could not resist it. 'The other one, Phil, Miss Femm——' she whispered.

He lowered his head. 'What about her?'

'She's a horror.'

Philip looked at her quickly, then pretended indignation. 'Well, that's a fine thing to say about your hostess.'

'No, I mean it, Phil. She's a horror. She makes me feel sick. I don't want to go near her.'

Philip was serious now. 'Why, what's she been doing?'

'Oh nothing, really. It's not that, it's just what she is. I'll tell you later.' Margaret turned round to find Mr. Femm almost at her elbow. Supper was ready, he told them.

The coldest of cold suppers awaited them on the table. There was the red ruin of a great joint of beef, a dish of cold potatoes, and plenty of bread, butter and cheese. Miss Femm, with her eyes narrowed and her mouth folded away, was already seated on the left-hand side. Philip and Margaret sat down on the near side; Mr. Femm seated himself opposite his sister; and Penderel marched round to the other side and sat down with his back to the front door. Morgan, looking more sullen than ever, hung about behind Miss Femm.

Philip looked round the table and fell to wondering. When he had first taken leave of the car and the rain and the darkness, his senses had been blunted and he had merely enjoyed, in a numb fashion, the shelter and the warmth and the feeling of security. Now his senses were sharp again and he began to tease himself with questions. Penderel caught his eye and grinned. This was Penderel's idea of a night, he told himself. It wasn't his. And then he suddenly admitted to himself that he didn't like this house and the people in it. These people had lived too long away from everybody and were now half crazy, and the house was musty with their mutual suspicion and resentment. Even Femm himself, who was at least civilised, was unsavoury in some queer way. Fine thoughts, these, for an uninvited guest about to diminish these people's small store of food.

'Tell me, Philip,' Margaret said, 'why these lights are so jumpy. They're getting on my nerves. They make everything look so unreal.'

'Evidently they make their own light here,' he told her,

pleasantly matter-of-fact. 'And there's something wrong with the batteries or the wiring. You can't be surprised, a night like this, whatever they do. So don't be alarmed if they go out altogether.'

Margaret nodded in silence. The thought of being left in total darkness filled her mind. Her skin tightened and shrank again from a clammy touch. If those lights did go out, she wouldn't move a yard from the fire and Philip until morning.

Mr. Femm, who had exchanged a remark with Penderel, now remembered his duties as a host and stretched a hand towards the dish of potatoes.

'Stop!' screamed his sister, making them all jump. 'What are you doing? We're not all heathens.'

He brought back his hand, folded his arms, and looked across at her with a sneer on his face. Then he glanced at the others and spoke to them in a voice that was out of reach of her ears. 'I had forgotten that my sister, who is nothing if not a good Christian, would want to ask a blessing. We shall enjoy our food so much more once she has called the attention of her tribal deity to us.'

'Horace Femm,' she cried across the table, 'you're blaspheming. If I can't hear, I can see. There's blasphemy written across your face.'

He leaned forward and used that curious hissing voice which they had noticed before. 'My dear Rebecca, I was merely telling your guests, who were wondering why they were not being served, that you were about to ask a blessing, to thank God for His bounty and His mercy, for this ample and delectable supper——'

'That will do,' she screamed at him. 'I know your mocking, lying tongue.'

'——For the health and prosperity and happiness granted to this family, for these years of peace and plenty, for all our pleasant days and quiet nights. Thank Him not only for yourself but for me, and for Roderick, and for Saul——'

'Stop, you fool!' She threw out her hand as she yelled and

glared at him across the table, and immediately the spirit, which had made his voice drop wormwood, died out of him. He looked confused and frightened, and sank back into his chair. There followed a moment's silence. They were all little frozen figures. Then Miss Femm bent her head and gabbled a grace.

'You think you're safe now, Horace, and you've had something to drink.' She was busy filling the plates at her side with slices of beef, and she spoke more quietly. 'And now you think you can afford to let that bad tongue of yours wag again. You'll be sorry you didn't keep it still.'

He roused himself. 'I am sorry I have had a hand in this ridiculous scene,' he told her. Then he turned to Margaret and showed her the ghost of a smile. 'I must apologise for these exhibitions of—what shall I say?—rural eccentricities. We have lived so long alone here that we have forgotten how to behave in front of visitors. Even I, who only returned here during the War and have known the world, have forgotten my manners. We are old and rusty mountain hermits. You must excuse us.'

This was as embarrassing as the rest of it, and Margaret was glad to busy herself with the potatoes that he somewhat fantastically proffered with his apology. Philip and Penderel, having exchanged glances across the width of the table, said nothing but tried to be bustling with plates and slices of bread and the cruet. Good old eating, thought Penderel, it'll carry anything off. Not that he minded these little family quarrels of the Femms, he told himself; he rather enjoyed them. They were like a passage from a new kind of morality play; a short scene for the sneering bone and the screaming flesh.

Nobody spoke. It was one of those silences not easily broken; their strength is tested by a tap or two of words tried over in the mind, and then they are left alone. Margaret bent over her plate. Philip was idly watching Miss Femm, who was heaping red meat on the plate that Morgan held out to her. The man looked so huge and savage that it seemed strange to see him with a plate at all. He ought to have taken the joint itself in his hairy hands and retired mumbling into a corner to gnaw it. Philip turned to his supper, and wondered who would speak next.

In another moment he was answered. The whole world spoke next. What happened was the last thing that any of them expected to happen. They all jumped and looked towards the door, now clamourous with repeated and urgent rappings.

'What's that?' cried Miss Femm. 'The door?'

'Yes,' roared Penderel, enjoying the sound of his own voice. 'There's someone outside.'

'They can't come in,' she shrieked.

'Who can it be?' Mr. Femm looked from one to the other and his voice quavered.

Penderel answered him. 'More visitors. Benighted, like us.' He looked across at Waverton and grinned.

'They can't come in,' Miss Femm shrieked again.

This angered Philip and he found his voice. 'That's what they are, I expect,' he told Mr. Femm. 'You'll have to let them in, of course. It's probably dangerous to be out now.'

The knocking had stopped now. There was a faint sound of voices. Mr. Femm glanced rapidly from Philip to his sister. Then the knocking began again.

Penderel stood up. 'The poor beggars must be half drowned. We can't keep them waiting there.'

'No, we shall have to let them in.' Mr. Femm bent forward and looked at his sister. 'Of course they will have to come in, if they want shelter. Morgan, go and open the door.'

Miss Femm pushed back her chair and looked up at Morgan. 'Go on then,' she cried, pointing to the door. 'And I'll come with you and see who they are.' Morgan lumbered forward and very slowly drew back the bolts. When he had opened the door an inch or two so that Miss Femm might peer out, it was unexpectedly thrown wide open and someone came in, pushing past the two at the door. It was a girl, all wet and muddy. She came further into the room, stopped to draw a long breath, then threw herself into the nearest chair and cried: 'My God! What a night!'

She was followed by a bulky middle-aged man, equally wet and muddy. For a moment he stood there looking about him and gasping for breath. Then he removed his dripping hat and showed them a ruddy face with a heavy shaven jowl. 'Thought you were never going to open that door. Never knew such a night. There's a reservoir burst or something and a big land-slide. Smashed my car and only just got away with our lives. Doubt if you're safe here. Phew!' He mopped his face and then looked from one to another of them. 'Sorry to barge in like this, but you see how it is. Who's the owner here?'

Philip suddenly recognised the man. 'Why,' he cried, step-ping forward, 'surely you're Sir William Porterhouse? I thought so. I'm Waverton, of Treffield and Waverton, architects. You once called to see us about something.'

'So I did.' Sir William extended a hand. 'I remember you now. This your place?'

Philip explained the situation and everybody was intro-duced. The girl was presented to them as Miss Gladys Du Cane. She had now taken off her hat and coat and stood revealed as a very pretty girl in her early twenties. She was slightly below medium height (an inch or two shorter than Margaret) and squarely though finely built. Her hair was thick and dark and crisp, and she had full hazel eyes, and a wide-lipped scarlet mouth setting off a rather pale face. Margaret decided at once that the girl belonged to a type that she detested. It was curious to see her here, so far from Shaftesbury Avenue and the lights and the dance bands and the theatres and the film agencies that were her obvious background. It was just as if an electric sign had found its way into the room. But these two people, insufferable though they might be in other circum-stances, were not unwelcome. They made everything seem less fantastic and mysterious and unbearable.

'No telephone here, I suppose?' Sir William had turned to Mr. Femm.

'No telephone or any other sign and mark of civilisation,' Mr. Femm told him. 'You are now completely cut off from the world, sir, but apparently this house will not suffer from the floods and the landslides.'

'The road must have gone completely at each side now,' said Philip. He remembered how he had resented the magnate's super-man airs in town, and found a certain malicious pleasure now in the sight of his helplessness. It would do him good. 'It was impassable when we came here, three-quarters of an hour ago. I can't imagine how you got here at all.'

'We must have been just behind you.' Sir William found a chair and drew up to the table. 'Think I saw your lights once. I pressed on, no good going back, and found myself in a devil of a situation. Car was nearly under water, stopped, started again, stopped again, then ran into a landslide or something of that sort. The bonnet was hit by a flying rock, the wheels were stuck, and in a minute the car was half buried. Took us all our time to get out.'

'How did you find this place?' Philip asked him.

'Left the car there. It's there now if it hasn't been washed into the valley—damn shame, too—it's a little Hispano I had made specially, to drive myself—only car I ever cared about. Always the same though, care about a thing and it's done in before you can say "knife." Well, we crawled out and didn't know where we were. Pitch black and raining like fury and water spouting all over the place. Had to leave everything, bags and all. No use going back, I said, we hadn't passed a light or signs of a house for miles. We went on, sloshing in mud, up to the knees in water, climbing over rocks. We'd an electric torch, but that wasn't much good. Then we saw a light and made for it as best we could. And here we are, and here we'll have to stay, at least till morning and perhaps longer. It's getting worse out there. You'd think it was the end of the world after being out in it for ten minutes; I don't mind telling you I thought I was nearly through. Can I use this glass?' He produced a flask from his pocket, emptied it into the glass, and promptly swallowed the inch of whisky in one gulp.

'Hello!' his late companion called across. 'You've not finished it, have you?'

'Afraid I have, Gladys.' And he showed her the flask.

'Well, I must say, Bill, you are a pig.' And the girl made a face when he threw her a rather perfunctory 'Sorry.' She was now sitting close to the fire and, having pulled off the high boots she had been wearing, was holding out one steaming silk-stockinged foot after another near the blaze.

'I've got a pair of slippers with me that I had in the car,' she confided to Margaret, 'and that's all I have got. What a night! I'll bet you had it pretty rough, didn't you?'

'Yes, it was very bad,' Margaret answered indifferently.

'Well, we're out of it now all right unless this place is swamped during the night.' Then she lowered her voice. 'Any beds going?'

Margaret shook her head. 'No, we shall have to stay in here all night.' Her voice sounded stiff, unfriendly, and that was a pity perhaps, but really she couldn't help it. She had spent years disliking the type at a distance and she couldn't change in a few minutes just because this obvious week-ending chorus girl had chanced to come under the same roof, out of the same wild night. The man was different. She didn't mind him. Indeed, his very bluffness and vulgarity would be useful here, breeding a coarse sanity in this queer situation.

They were returning to supper now. Morgan had lurched off with his plate, and the others were settling down again at the table. The baronet confessed that he was ready for some cold meat and bread and cheese, and had found a place between Margaret and Mr. Femm. 'Come along, Gladys,' he called, 'if you want something to eat. We interrupted this little supper party and we've been asked to join it.'

'Righto,' she cried. 'I'm coming.' And Penderel brought up a chair for her and she sat down by his side. He noticed that she met the long stare of Miss Femm, now so much folded and silent fat, with a smile that was deliciously near a grin. It wasn't mere cheek either. This girl was all right.

She looked at him frowningly. 'What's your name? Sorry, but I can never remember.'

'Penderel.' And that's the worst of being nobody in particular, he thought, for you always feel a fool when you bring out your name.

She frowned at him again. 'What else? 'Scuse me asking.'

'Roger,' he told her, and thought it sounded rusty. It was some time since he heard it.

'Roger Penderel.' She was obviously turning it over in her mind. 'Look here, don't you know a boy called Ranger, Dick Ranger?'

'Lord, yes. I know young Ranger. His elder brother, Tom, used to be a great pal of mine. He's somewhere in the Sudan now, being done to a turn. Dick's not been down long from Oxford and has developed into a tremendous West Ender. He knows all the places, stops out late, and is as cynical as a taxi driver. He quite frightens me, makes me feel old and simple.'

'I know him too,' she said. 'He's rather a nice boy really, bit young and silly of course. I asked because I'm sure I saw you with him once. I knew I'd seen you somewhere and I couldn't think where, but now I remember. Weren't you with him one night—three or four months ago—at the "Rats and Mice"?'

'The "Rats and Mice"?' Then he remembered the place, one of the smaller night clubs. 'Yes, I did go there one night with Dick Ranger. It's a little place, isn't it, with everything and everybody jammed together. There was a band all squashed in a balcony, just like sardines in a half-opened tin. I remember the name of the place because I told Ranger it was like being inside a cheese. I hated it. The drinks were about the worst and the dearest I've ever known.'

'Pretty rotten, yes, but not quite so bad if you're in with the crowd who are running it. I go there a lot, though it's not my favourite haunt.'

'Haunt's a good word, isn't it?' He grinned at her and she—

perhaps mechanically, he didn't know—wrinkled her nose in reply. 'We have to go somewhere, haven't we?'

'That's just it. That's what I always say.' She was quite eager about this. 'You can have a dance or two and a drink with some of the girls and boys you know, and the band's making a cheerful row and the lights are nice and bright, and so you turn in there night after night and hang on, not wanting to turn out and crawl home to your rotten digs.'

'I know. Once down the steps and outside the door, it's dark and raining probably and to-morrow's begun. So you put it off.'

'You've hit it in one,' she told him. And then, after a moment's reflection, she went on: 'It's like being in here after that.' She jerked her head towards the door. Then she lowered her voice. 'This seems a funny, dingy sort of hole—funny people here too—but it's the Ritz itself after being out there.'

'Yes, I suppose it is.' He didn't want to sound dubious, but he couldn't help wondering. He turned his glance on the impassive Miss Femm for a moment, then looked across at her brother, who was talking to Porterhouse.

'You surprise me, sir,' Mr. Femm was remarking, though there was no surprise but something quite different flickering in his eyes. 'But then, I have been out of the world, you might say, for at least ten years. I never even see a newspaper now.'

'You wouldn't know it, then. Take my word for that,' said Porterhouse. 'You couldn't come back into it. It's a different world altogether. I've kept pace with it, so to speak; might even say I've been in front; but it's taken me all my time.'

'The world will be very different,' said Mr. Femm, slowly, 'when all the people have been cleared out of it, and not before. Men and women do not change. Their silly antics are always the same. There will always be a few clever ones, who can see a yard or two in front of their noses, and a host of fools who can see nothing, who are all befuddled, who pride themselves on being virtuous because they are incompetent or short-sighted.'

'Something in that, p'r'aps,' the other admitted, after a stare.

Margaret Waverton was talking to her husband. Her rather clipped and very clear voice found its way across the table. 'But you'll never get Muriel Ainsley to see that, Philip. It's really astonishing how people, people with brains too, can know so little about themselves. The more I see of life, the more I'm convinced that onlookers really do see most of the game.'

'So they do.' Philip's voice, dropping into a meditative bass, could be heard distinctly. 'Only life isn't a game, you know, and you never really feel it is except where you yourself are not concerned. That's where the smart saying breaks down; nearly all smart sayings do break down badly. Anyhow, we ought to stop talking about life, because what we say doesn't mean anything. What's the use of saying it's like this or means that, when obviously it includes both this and that and their opposites.'

'Don't be sententious, Philip,' she told him. 'You've said that before, too. Besides, I was talking about Muriel Ainsley.'

But they were all sententious, Penderel reflected, himself included. They were settling down very cosily. They would all start boasting soon, and if he wasn't careful, he would be the first, though as usual he would do it topsy-turvily. It was odd how what you might call the Femmishness of the place had suddenly vanished—no, not vanished but retreated. He thought of the girl at his side. Certainly it didn't stand much of a chance with her, this Femmishness. But perhaps it hadn't fairly begun yet. He had a feeling that there was more to come. There was a whole night before them and it was early yet. Why, the little band wouldn't have arrived yet at the 'Rats and Mice.'

CHAPTER V

They had finished eating now and had somehow drifted into silence. Throughout supper, all six of them (Miss Femm had never spoken a word) had chatted easily, though there had been no general burst of talk; but now they were quiet. They might have been waiting for a signal, they were so curiously still. Then suddenly they were given one, for Miss Femm, who had begun to seem a mere object, turned herself into a real person again by rising from her chair and waddling away. She said nothing, gave no meaning glances, did not hesitate, but simply arose and departed. From her manner, they might have been as unreal to her as she had been to them. They stared after her in silence. If they were waiting for a signal, it was not this.

There came a second one, this time out of the encompassing night, which they had almost forgotten. It might have been thunder rolling among the hills, the bursting of a bank above, or another landslide; the noise was distant and indeterminate, and yet it was full of menace. Sharply, dramatically, it pointed to their situation, like a pin stuck into a map. The roof and walls were no longer another sky and horizon but were roof and walls and nothing more. A little box held them all, tiny creatures crouching in a dot of light. Thus dwarfed and huddled together in body, their spirits first shrank to a point and then expanded in concert. They awoke to share a common mood. The change in them was as decisive as Miss Femm's exit, but it had to struggle through to the surface, into speech, and so it seemed gradual, as if curtain after curtain of gauze were being raised between them.

Philip made the first remark, and all he said was: 'If nobody objects, I think I'll have a pipe.' That was nothing, yet by addressing the whole company as he did, he made it easier for the others to speak to the whole table. He brought out his pipe, Sir William found a cigar, and Penderel and the two women lit cigarettes. Mr. Femm contented himself with gin-and-water.

'You know,' said Penderel, 'we ought to play a game.'

'Good idea,' cried Sir William, very hearty and masterful behind his cigar. 'Can't sleep yet. What about bridge?'

Margaret jumped at this. 'I'd love a game.' She thought how comforting the familiar faces of the kings and queens would be. No wonder old people, surrounded by strange faces and passing Death every night on the stairs, became so passionately fond of cards.

'But I've no cards,' Sir William went on. He turned to Mr. Femm. 'Expect you've got a pack of cards you could lend us, eh?'

'I have none myself,' Mr. Femm began, 'but I have seen a pack here——' He stopped short, something came and went in his eyes, then he shook his head hastily. 'No, there are none here. I am sorry.' It was very queer. Penderel, remembering, looked at him curiously and began to wonder again. Sir William appealed to the Wavertons, but they had none.

'We'll play Truth,' said Penderel. 'It's just the moment for it.'

'So they have turned it into a game now, have they?' cried Mr. Femm, in his thin, bitter voice. 'It was high time they did.'

Sir William looked puzzled. 'Don't seem to know it, and don't like the sound of it. How d'you play it? Hope it isn't one of those games that make you use paper and pencil, like so many kids at school. If it is, you can count me out. I hate 'em.'

'So do I,' cried Gladys. 'Is it one of them?'

'It's the simplest game in the world,' Penderel explained. 'Indeed you can hardly call it a game. We just go on talking but we stop lying. We simply ask one another questions, and these questions must be answered truthfully. You have to be on your honour to answer as truthfully as you can.'

'My God!' Gladys couldn't help it, but she stopped short and then said 'Sorry!'

'This doesn't seem to be your game, Gladys,' Sir William told her. 'You'd better keep out.'

She shook her head very decisively. 'Not me. I'm on. It'll be a nice change for some of us, you particularly, Bill. But somebody wants to be easy with the questions, or God knows what we shall hear.' She darted a glance across the table at Margaret to see how she was taking it. Not too well apparently. Serve her right.

'You two are in?' Penderel looked at the Wavertons and they nodded. 'We're all in, then. Now, don't forget, you're bound to answer as truthfully as you can. Get down to the stony facts.'

'When you think of it,' Philip growled, looking down into his pipe, 'the very existence of this pastime, with its one rule about answering truthfully, is an awful comment on society.'

Mr. Femm stared at him. 'But what do you expect?'

'Couldn't say what we think all the time or there'd'—and Sir William waved his cigar—'there'd be the devil to pay! Not sure how it'll work even here. Still, I'm with you, and I promise to tell the truth. Won't hurt me for once. D'you all promise?' They all promised.

'How shall we begin, then?' asked Margaret. It was queer, but she was quite eager to begin. She had played it before and had hated it—a thoroughly mischievous little game, she had thought. But now, perhaps because she was in such an odd jumble of a company, perhaps because she was simply taking shelter here, she was more than willing to ask and answer and listen.

'We'll do it this way,' Penderel suggested. He pointed to Waverton. 'I'll ask you a question, then you'll ask Mrs. Waverton, and so on round the table. That's a pleasant neighbourly way of doing it. But everyone must speak up so that we can all hear.'

Nobody objected to the arrangement. 'Ask away, then,' said Philip. 'But don't be too hard on me. Remember I'm a shy man and I'm the first in the confessional.'

'All right. Nothing too searching to begin with.' Penderel

reflected for a moment. 'How's this, then? There are, you'll agree, innumerable snags in life——'

'Oh, you mustn't talk to him about life,' Margaret broke in. 'He's just told me not to.'

'You be quiet, Margaret,' Philip growled, but felt himself warming towards her. That little characteristic thrust suddenly and cosily domesticated them. 'Yes,' he told Penderel, 'I admit the snags.'

'Good. Well, then'—and Penderel rumpled his hair and the girl at his side laughed at him—'tell us what seems to you the snag-in-chief, the great, the fundamental snag. In a word, if there's a catch in life, where does the catch come in? You follow me? Name the fly in the ointment.'

Philip puffed at his pipe. 'Wait a minute. That's a question that can't be answered without thought.' He puffed away again.

'You see what I mean?' said Penderel. 'Of course, you may not think there is any one great snag or catch. If so, you simply say so.'

'I wish I could,' Philip replied. 'I can't, though, because there is a catch, an enormous fly in the ointment. And to me, it's this. It seems to me that life demands so much care to be lived at all decently that it's hardly worth living. I'm talking about life as we see it, civilisation as it's called, and not the life, say, of a Fiji Islander or a Zulu. With us the whole thing has got to be so careful, so ordered, has become so conscious, asks for so much planning and safeguarding, that we never arrive at any real enjoyment or ease, to say nothing of sheer rapture. We're like people walking on a tightrope, and the only real pleasure we get is when we say to ourselves, "Well, that bit's safely passed." Do you see what I mean? If you decide to lean back and enjoy things, then you simply come a cropper and everything's smashed for you; but if you're careful to avoid the cropper, it takes so much out of you that you can't really enjoy life at all. And it's no use talking about the golden mean and compromise and so forth, because if you try to work on that principle, you only get bits of cropper, bits of anxiety and carefulness, bits of cropper again, a miserable alternation. If you let things go at all, disaster comes; if you don't, if you look after them, then you're simply working hard at it all the time. The trouble is that we can't trust life, and in order to keep going with it at all, we have to be for ever watching it and patching it up. Therefore the only sort of happiness we can get out of it is like the weird pleasure that some people get from making and altering and fiddling about with wireless sets. So long as we continually turn the discs and change coils, we can congratulate ourselves on the fact that the set's working, but that's all we can do. We can't sit back and listen to the music. There's the great snag. You all see what I mean?'

'Can't say that I do exactly,' said Sir William. 'Give me an instance.'

'Well, take a comparatively simple matter. Health, for example. Life's hardly worth living without decent health, but according to the thousand and one experts of the body, we must look after this and that and the other in order to keep reasonably fit, and if we took the slightest notice of one-half of them we should be worrying about our bodies all day. Most of us don't trouble, of course, but the fact remains that most of us are rapidly drifting further and further away from good health and we shall soon find ourselves crocked. I'd like to come to a life in which I could play the fool with my body without inevitable disaster. I must have been meant for such a life, for there's something inside me that protests against these conditions we know. Or, take personal relations. They ought to be delightfully easy and careless, but they can't be now that we're so self-conscious. The best of them can't be left to look after themselves a month, and to keep them going properly is only another anxiety. By the time our relations with the people close to us have been put in proper trim, we're in no state to enjoy them but can only find a dim sort of pleasure in the thought that they are in proper trim. Again, take children. Being a parent is rapidly becoming a nightmare of worry. I'm not attacking mere crankiness now, for most of the worry is justified, and that's the trouble. If you don't worry, if you are grand and complacent, then life will make haste to see that they suffer for it. You can't enjoy the children—you've no energy left for it—you can only enjoy repeating to yourself that you're doing your best for them. We've no easy and rapturous contact with things themselves; we only watch their shadows, either anxiously or, at the best, with a dim sense of triumph. There's the snag, the catch, then. We've either eaten too much or still too little from the Tree of Knowledge. As it is, we know just enough to give life a hair-trigger.' Then he looked round apologetically. 'Sorry. I seem to have made a speech.'

While the others were waving away his apology, Margaret was telling herself that she had never heard Philip reveal himself so clearly and fully, even though he did it unconsciously. That speech was dear old Phil all over: he didn't trust life an inch. It was a silly grumble, she told herself, but only the very nicest kind of man could have made it. And now it was her turn. She looked at Philip speculatively. What would he ask her?

'Your turn to ask now, Waverton,' said Penderel. 'And you're lucky, having a wife for victim.'

Philip looked at her as if she were a strange person. It gave Margaret a little thrill, though she knew that it was because they were playing this game, for she had noticed that look before in company.

'Your question is this,' said Philip, still looking at her as if he had hardly ever seen her before. 'What do you want? What are you getting at? What do you want, in your heart of hearts, to do, to be? What's the core of the thing for you?'

'That's the sort of question a man would ask,' Margaret exclaimed. 'As if I had a definite object in life tucked away in a pigeonhole in my mind! Still, I'll try to find an answer. Let me think.' She glanced round at the eyes fixed upon her, and wished there was another woman of her own kind there, to

whom she could address herself. That girl wouldn't understand. 'Well,' she began, hesitatingly, 'I'm not sure I can make
myself clear or whether you'll understand. The question is,
what am I getting at, what do I really want to do or to be, isn't
it? All I can say is that I want to create a certain atmosphere,
which I won't attempt to define for you. It's in my mind, just as
the idea for a novel or a play is in an author's mind, but I have to
bring it outside, into life—do you see?—just as the author has.
I want to bathe life itself in this atmosphere. I want to move in
the centre of this atmosphere, really to be always creating it,
and I want the people close to me, the ones I care for, to live in
this atmosphere, and other people, friendly outsiders, to come
and dip into it and recognise it and tell themselves that it's my
atmosphere and very good. This atmosphere contains all the
good things of life, all those things that men put into separate
compartments and somehow raise above life, and because it
includes them, is served by them, it's naturally more important than any of them.' She warmed to the thought now and
forgot her audience. 'By doing this—or trying to do this—
you're creating in the most marvellous way because you're
using life itself as the raw material. And the women who've
succeeded in doing it—there are bad atmospheres as well as
good ones, of course—are really tremendous, like queens
without the fuss and the show. Men only notice it in a dim sort
of way, though they're affected by it, of course, and you can
see how the greatest of them have been enchanted by a certain
woman's atmosphere. They've not simply fallen in love, as
people always think, but they've discovered a new country and
have stayed there. That's what I want then, to create my own
little country.' She stopped, breathless, and looked round at
her listeners, feeling suddenly frightened. The next moment
there would be a huge guffaw. But there wasn't; everybody
looked either puzzled or friendly or both; and she felt relieved
and rather happy. She smiled at them: 'I seem to have been
guilty of a speech too. I apologise.'

They cried out at this. 'No apologies necessary, Mrs.

Waverton,' Sir William's voice came booming. 'You're too deep for me, though. Who's next? Can't we have a few facts?'

It was Margaret's turn, and her neighbour was Mr. Femm. She looked at him in bewilderment. He ought not to have been included, she felt, as she stared at the long, lined yellow mask he turned to her. There were deep wrinkles all round his eyes and the thin high bridge of his nose gleamed white as if the bone had burst through the skin, but the eyes themselves were as vague as smoke. She couldn't ask him anything. He was as strange as a mandarin. Then she suddenly remembered Rebecca Femm and the dead Rachel Femm and the women who came in silks and scents and the men who said 'Go away and pray,' and it all seemed like something from a crazy old story she had just laid aside, and yet this man was in it, a character come to life. No, not quite to life.

'I am ready, Mrs. Waverton.' How queer it was to hear him speak. It made it worse.

'Hurry up, Margaret.' This from Philip. She was being absurd. Anything would do. 'Tell us,' she heard herself saying, 'why you chose to live here.'

Mr. Femm took a sip of his gin-and-water and replaced the glass very carefully, then he peered across the table, at the place his sister had vacated, and compressed his thin lips until his mouth seemed to vanish completely. 'I came here,' he said finally, 'or rather I returned here, for I was born and brought up in this very house, for the same reason that brought you here. I did not want to live again in this house just as you did not want to spend a night in it. You came here for shelter, and so did I. When I decided to return, I had no money and no further prospects, if only because I was wanted by the police. That surprises you. It was nothing really criminal, nothing, that is, in bad taste, but the Law in this country happens to be as heavy and stupid and idiotic as the poor creatures it is supposed to benefit, and Chance for once was not on my side. This is the home of my family, it was my home too, once, so I returned to it, knocked at the door as you did to-night and demanded shelter. I have been here ever since.' He lifted his glass again while they stared at him in silence. It was not that they were struck dumb by amazement but that there did not seem to be anything to say. Sir William made a noise in his throat that sounded like the preliminaries of speech, but he must have changed his mind for no words came.

'So far, so good,' said Penderel. 'It's your question now, Mr. Femm.' But he couldn't imagine that heavy-jowled magnate, whose turn it was, telling the truth. He was too rich, too successful, for the truth.

Mr. Femm glanced at his neighbour and then looked straight in front of him. 'You must tell us,' he said, slowly, 'the worst thing you have done during these last twelve months.'

'Here!' cried Sir William, protesting. 'That's a stinger, isn't it?'

'The thing,' Mr. Femm added calmly, 'that you are most ashamed of doing.'

'You don't want much, do you?' He blew out a cloud of cigar smoke as if to relieve his feelings. Then he considered. 'Well, I don't know.' He frowned and looked doubtful, but then suddenly his face cleared. 'All right. You shall have it. The worst thing I've done this year. It's nothing startling. Don't expect any Sunday paper stuff, amazing revelations, orgies in the West End, that sort of stuff. But I'll be honest with you; this really is the thing I'm most ashamed of. No names, of course, and all in confidence. Well, a few months ago I had a quarrel with the manager of one of my concerns and got rid of him. That's all. But there's a devil of a lot behind it. I said he wasn't good enough, didn't suit me, but the fact is he was one of the best managers I'd got and a better man than the fellow that took his place. And I knew it. He was just the sort of man I wanted in the business, a real find, all over the work and keen as a razor. But I booted him out. Why? I'll tell you.' He stopped for a moment, set his jaw, then laughed shortly. 'You'll probably find it amusing. I got rid of him because I couldn't stand his damned superiority. That's what it amounts to. He was only a youngster, had only left Oxford or Cambridge a few years when he came to me. He got to be manager of this particular concern in no time. I believe in rapid promotion and this fellow was worth it. But every time I saw him he made me uneasy. Nothing in his manner, at least nothing you could put a finger on. But—well, I always wanted to ask him where he got his shirts and ties from; I could never find any like 'em. That's nothing, you think, but it worried me, made me feel uneasy. Then one day he asked me to go to dinner, meet his wife, who'd be honoured and delighted and so on. I went, and that settled it. There were only the three of us. His wife was very charming, very pretty woman too, and talked well. Her father'd been the Professor of something-or-other at Edinburgh. She was obviously in love with her husband and he with her, really in love, and I know the difference. Well, that was all right, something I like to see, in fact, though you mightn't think it, but I'm a bit of a sentimentalist. They talked and they let me talk, encouraged me, were almost deferential. But that superiority was there. It was the shirts and ties all over again, only much worse. I felt more and more uncomfortable, uneasy, dissatisfied somehow. I tried to talk the feeling down, told 'em some of the things I'd done, spread myself out, but I knew it was just missing all the time. I could hear my own voice going on and on, bragging to no purpose; I could see myself, hot and sweating and waving my arms; and yet I knew this wasn't really myself, you know. There was something in the confounded atmosphere of these people that was making me publish a libel of myself just to make some sort of impression on them. And the harder I tried, the more I was convinced that what I was saying, what I did, what I looked like, didn't amount to anything, that is, didn't seem to amount to anything with these people. D'you see what I mean? Of course I knew well enough, nobody better, that it did amount to something; I don't pretend to despise myself. But I couldn't get it over, as the actors say. And while I was fuming and sweating and talking big, there they sat, absolutely easy and comfortable, so damned sure of themselves. Nothing to do with social experience, y'know, for I'd had as much of that as they had. I'd had more, been to places they hadn't reached, not by a long chalk. It was that mysterious superiority. Well, when I couldn't make any headway against it, it got on my nerves. I'd beat it somehow. So when I left them that night, I said to myself, going home, "All right. I'll show you. You're doing very well, aren't you? Everything's beautiful. Well, we'll see. I've made you and I'll unmake you." Within a month I'd faked a lot of grievances against him, and very soon I had him out. I paid for it, of course, losing a good man. It was all dead against my own interests. But I couldn't rest until I'd done it. But I knew what I'd done. A damned dirty trick, weak too. And that's that. Gad, but I'm thirsty.'

He accepted some of Mr. Femm's gin, the only drink on hand, hastily mixed it with water, and, without lifting his eyes, emptied the glass. 'That's better,' he said, and looked round. If they didn't like it, he thought, they could lump it. Anyhow, they had asked him and he had told them the truth. He had rather enjoyed it too; this was the time and place for telling these things, explaining yourself for once in a while. It was all right; they all looked just curious and friendly, except perhaps the one person he knew, Gladys. She was looking a bit scornful (as she always said herself), not so friendly as the other girl, Mrs. Waverton, who had seemed so cool and superior at first. But then Gladys was probably not judging the case but merely happened to be out of patience with him.

'Your turn to answer now, Miss Du Cane,' Penderel told her. 'You're in this, of course?'

Yes, she was in it, and looked eagerly at Sir William. 'Come on,' she cried, 'let's know the worst.'

'So it's your turn, Miss Du Cane, is it?' Sir William smiled rather grimly at her. The name itself suggested a question to him. 'Suppose, then, you tell us exactly who you are.'

'Well, if you're not the limit!' There was real anger in her fine eyes. 'What d'you mean by your "exactly who you are"?'

The others felt uncomfortable, but Sir William himself was not disturbed. 'Nothing in that. I mean, give us a few biographical details, the sort of thing you find in "Who's Who." Think of the question I had to answer. Yours is easy.' But there was a touch of malice in the smile he gave her.

Gladys stared at him, pushing out her full underlip, then gave a slight shrug and leaned back in her chair. 'All right then. Here goes.' But she stopped for a moment and looked in front of her with unseeing eyes. Then she seemed to give herself a little shake, lifted her chin, and spoke out briskly and bravely. 'Well, to begin with my name's not Du Cane. Probably none of you thought it really was, but that doesn't make it easier to say right out that it isn't. My real name's Hoskiss; the Gladys is all right. When I first thought of trying to get into the chorus, I wanted another name, and I happened to see a book called "The Expensive Miss Du Cane." That's me, I thought. I was only a kid, seventeen about, at the time. We lived down in Fulham, Walham Green, to be exact, just off North End Road. There were seven of us, three girls, two boys, and mother and father. Father's a joiner, when he's working. I don't suppose any of you know North End Road and district. You should go and have a look at it some time. It's not one of these absolutely poverty-stricken places, and it strikes you as being quite cheery, lively in fact—so long as you're half tight or don't have to live there. I used to run up and down North End Road fetching fried fish and bottles of stout for the family, and try to make enough to get into the gallery of the Granville—that's the little music-hall at the bottom. We'd only got half a house for the whole seven of us, and the house itself was no size at all, and we were always in one another's way, with everybody grousing and nagging like fury. We'd one little room for the three of us, the girls I mean, and you can imagine what that was like, each of us shoving the others' things out of the way or borrowing them to go out in. I was always doing that, being the youngest. Maggie, my eldest sister, got a job as a waitress, met a soldier on leave she liked who said he'd marry her when

the war was over. She had a baby and he never came back, and
that was that. The kid's at home now and Maggie's still a waitress, though not at the same place. Ethel, the one next to me,
went to work in a laundry and then got married, married to
something that looks like a rat and acts like one. The only thing
you could say in his favour was that he was a great change after
a laundry. Then I had to go out and work, and went through
job after job, three months in one of those cheap sweet shops
run by a dirty little Jew who was always putting his arm round
me, another three months running about in a big draper's,
running round from morning till night, till I was fit to drop,
then in other shops till I landed in the pictures, odd-job girl at
one of the local picture palaces. That suited me all right, and at
first I thought no end of myself, but the money was rotten, the
manager got too friendly, and I couldn't stick being at home.
After I'd been an hour in that house, I wanted to scream. Every
time I went up West—to see a show at Daly's or the Gaiety or
the Palace or the Palladium—I'd be awake half the night. And
then one night I went to the Granville with two girls I knew
and some boys, and they took us into the bar at the interval
and gave us some port, and some people from the show came
in and we all got friendly. One of the girls had dropped out
of that show—it was a revue called "Oh, my eye!" absolutely
fifteenth rate—and I dropped in. They'd been playing at some
of the little London halls and were now going down into the
country on one of the bread-and-dripping tours, you know
the sort, All This Week in the Pier Pavilion or Three Nights
Only at the Corn Exchange. I went with 'em, Miss Du Cane,
third from the right in the chorus of twelve. And that's how
Gladys left home.'

'Ever been back since?' asked Sir William.

'Course I have. But not to live, not likely. I used to look in
sometimes when I was flush, and take something for mother
or Maggie's kid. I like 'em all and they like me. If you take
any one of them away, get them into a quiet corner away
from home and the others, put a drink in front of them, they

come out then, you really get to know them. It's when they're all jumbled up together at home, nagging and grousing and snarling, that they get on your nerves, at least on mine.' She looked across and met Margaret's level glance. 'But that's enough of that. I'm not going to tell the story of my life, sir, not even to-night when we're all lost and far from home and Piccadilly Circus seems to be somewhere in New Zealand.'

'Well, ask a question then,' said Sir William. 'Get your own back.' He was enjoying this and was wondering what Gladys would demand of the rather pale but bright-eyed youngster on her right, Penderel, with whom she seemed to have struck up a friendship at once.

Gladys leaned forward and then turned her head so that she could look Penderel almost squarely in the face. He was telling himself that her eyes were like very old brown sherry, when she brought out her question. 'What are you so bitter about?'

'Me!' It had taken his breath away.

'Yes, you.' She nodded at him like a wise child.

'Why, am I bitter?'

'I think you are,' she told him. She appealed to the Wavertons.

'I know what you mean,' said Margaret. 'It's not perhaps the exact word, but it will do.' Then she addressed herself to Penderel: 'Yes, you are bitter, you know.'

'Of course you are, Penderel,' said Philip heartily. 'You're one of the worst post-War cases I know, a thundering sight worse than I am. Come on, admit it. You're the sort of bloke they denounce in little talks in Bright Sunday Evening Services.' He grinned and pointed his pipe-stem across the table. 'Stand up to your question and explain the wormwood.'

Penderel made a comical little grimace. 'Well, I never knew I was so obvious. I suppose I shall have to explain myself. I went into the War when I was seventeen, ran away from school to do it, enlisting as a Tommy and telling them I was nineteen. I'm not going to talk about the War. You know all about that. It killed my father, who died from over-work. It

killed my elder brother, Jim, who was blown to pieces up
at Passchendaele. He was the best fellow in the world, and
I idolised him. It was always fellows like him, the salt of the
earth, who got done in, whether they were British or French
or German or American. People wonder what's the matter
with the world these days. They forget that all the best fellows,
the men who'd have been in their prime now, who'd have been
giving us a lead in everything, are dead. If you could bring 'em
all back, fellows like Jim, hundreds and hundreds of thousands
of 'em, you'd soon see the difference they'd make in the place.
But they're dead, and a lot of other people, very different sort
of people, are alive and kicking. Well, I saw all this, took an
honours course in it, you might say, for it was the only educa-
tion I got after the fifth form. Then towards the end of the
War I fell in love. I was convalescent in a country house and
it was spring. She was staying there, and every time we went
out walking every little gust of wind snowed down blossom
on us. I've never seen a place so thick with apple blossom and
cherry blossom. And she'd be waiting down there. We became
engaged. The world was all made over again and I'd only got
to see the War through to find it all waiting for me. I thought
about nothing else, went back to France, went through the
dust and the gas of the last push in the summer and autumn
of 'eighteen, thinking about nothing else. Then just after the
Armistice I got a letter. It was all a mistake; we weren't really
suited, too young to know then; she'd found someone else;
we'd always be friends. All very reasonable, no doubt, but you
see I'd been thinking about nothing else. I got out of the Army,
went home and saw her once, and gave it up. But I remember
I went down to the old place that spring, in 'nineteen, and
all the damned blossom was out again, miles of it, snowing
through the air as it did before. It made me ache to see it. I told
myself that it hadn't been there for me and only another kind
of frost would stop it. I packed my traps and set off to look for
work.' He stopped and looked down at his fingers drumming
on the table.

'Go on,' said Philip, after they had waited a few moments. For that he received one of Margaret's fierce little nudges, always so surprising because they never seemed part of her. They belonged, in fact, to the other Margaret, the one inside. This was the first he had had for some months and it was so welcome that it tingled.

'I'll cut it short,' said Penderel. 'Well, the good fellows were nearly all gone, love was off, and the world was in a filthy muddle, but there was still work. That was the thing. I told myself I'd work like hell. I could have gone up to Oxford or Cambridge, but didn't want to go. I wasn't in the mood for listening to the patter of dry little men in spectacles and then going ragging with a lot of kids. I felt there was nothing a varsity could teach me that I wanted to learn. Pure arrogance, of course, but there you are. I didn't even want to play their games, their solemn good-form games. I'd go and work, find a man's job. There was an African scheme going, good land for ex-officers and all that, and so I scraped together every penny I had and went into it and out to Africa. I won't bore you with that. It was a swindle, and a particularly dirty swindle, the kind that sticks in your gullet. Africa didn't want me, at least the part I saw didn't, and I came back broke. I drifted about town for some time and swapped drinks with other fellows in the same boat. The work idea was off, but I was still looking for a job, which isn't the same thing at all though. One or two of the fellows I knew joined the Black and Tans, and I nearly joined myself—nobody else seemed to want me—but I happened to like the Irish and I didn't like the sound of their prospective job. So I hung about, talking over schemes with other drifters and having too many drinks. I sold one or two things on commission but found it a poor, dirty game. Then I found I hadn't a bean, didn't want to borrow, so put in a spell of navvying, up North on some public works, got the job through pure influence. That did me good, but I haven't the navvy temperament and technique and it was about as hard as a spell of penal servitude. But I stuck it till we were paid off, came back to town and went round the bars, seeing if there was anything doing. There was—there always is, if you've got the stomach for it—but I couldn't do it. I tried to write—I'd got plenty of material—but could only make a rotten hack job of it, just spoiling the stuff. Then my mother died. She'd not had much to live for after father and Jim went. My one sister had married and was out in India, and I wasn't exactly a howling success as the prop and mainstay of the family. Some money came to me. It wasn't much and it didn't last long. I've seen to that. There's still a little tied up, but I've borrowed on the strength of that. When you've nothing to do, no aim of any kind, very few real friends, money doesn't last long. There are twenty-four hours in every day to be paid for, bought off, you might say. I'm one of the ugly ducklings of the War generation, the sort that will never become swans. Already another generation's come up, who understand this world, who don't let it take them in, kids soft enough in body and speech but really as hard as nails, all out for a damned good time. They know what they want and how to get it, and nothing's going to take them in. I'm out too for a damned good time—there's nothing else to be out for, nothing left—but I don't get it. And I never will.'

He looked round at the faces turned to his. Mr. Femm appeared impassive, Sir William slightly uncomfortable, and the Wavertons and Gladys serious and sympathetic. Then suddenly he started up and broke into speech again, this time swiftly, vehemently.

'You think I've justified myself,' he cried to them. 'I haven't really. It's cant, though not the worst kind, but still it's cant. It's weak sentimentality merely turned topsy-turvy. I've realised that when I've heard other fellows explaining away their slackness. It's nearly as bad as being one of those creatures who, when they get put into the dock, begin snivelling about their War record. It's not the first time that boys have left school to be shot at, have lost their brothers and friends, have been jilted, have been swindled. If a man's got guts, he ought to be able to win through. That's what you ought to tell me. I know it. I know this disillusion or cynicism or bitterness or whatever it is is the new cant, an attitude, weakness trying to disguise itself. And that makes it worse for me. I say I ought to be able to win through, and then I ask myself "win through to what?" I don't like being in this pit, but there's no motive-power to lift me out, or you might say there isn't even any "out." You can put it another way. I asked Waverton what he thought was the great snag in life, the catch in it. I asked that because I was curious. I wondered if his idea would agree with mine. But it didn't. Mine's this. If you approach life in the old noble-silly fashion, then it'll simply cheat you and bump you badly. If you don't, if you crawl into it with no grand illusions, then you'll come to terms with it, of course, and live easily, but you'll be nothing but a pig, and it's not worth having at all on those terms.'

'That's not unlike mine, you know,' said Philip. 'Only I feel I could patch up your trouble, that a compromise is possible.'

'And that's what I felt about yours,' cried Penderel. 'I felt it would be possible to find a safe seat somewhere between the horns of your dilemma, but not between those of mine. Of course, if you're a born pig, you don't feel it, but if you've merely turned piggy, it hurts for a time. I'm hoping it'll stop hurting soon. I've turned piggy, of course.'

'You're a raging idealist,' Margaret smiled at him, 'or you wouldn't talk like that.'

'That's it,' said Sir William, complacent now. 'He wants the moon.'

'No, that's wrong,' replied Penderel, eagerly. 'That's something quite different. I know people like that, but if you think I am, you've missed the point.'

'I don't know, Penderel,' said Philip. 'Surely it's really a matter of wanting better bread than can be made of wheat, as someone once said of somebody.'

'No, it isn't.' Penderel was very emphatic. 'It's worse than that. It's finding that bread made out of wheat isn't worth eating.'

'That's the same thing,' Philip told him.

'I don't mean it to be.' He leaned forward on his elbow and frowned. 'Wait a minute and I'll tell you what I mean.'

'I know what you mean.' Gladys's voice surprised them all, for somehow they had not expected her to speak. 'Well, if I don't know what you mean, I know what's the matter with you. You've nothing to live for. You're just passing the time and it's rotten. Everything so far's been a washout, and now it's Monday morning all the week.'

Both Penderel and Sir William opened their mouths to speak, but they were drowned by a new voice that was so shrill and unexpected that it startled them all. Miss Femm had returned and was approaching the table, shrieking at her brother.

'Morgan's at the bottle again,' she was shrieking. 'I knew he'd begin to-night. Where did he get it from?'

Mr. Femm bit his lips. 'He did not get it from me. Can't you stop him?'

'There's no stopping him now. He's there in the kitchen, stupid already. I'll take these things away, the rest can stop where they are.' And she bore away the remains of the joint and the cheese.

The others pushed back their chairs and rose to their feet. That entrance had obviously put an end to their talk, during which they had seemed to be sitting on a bank, watching life go by like a river and pointing out to one another its eddies and ripples and gleams; but now, with the opening of a door and the sound of another voice, life seemed to be roaring round them again; they were in the river.

Miss Femm was back again. 'If he goes on, he'll have to be watched,' she screamed. 'It's getting worse outside too. We've not done with it yet.' She departed with the bread and the butter.

Sir William felt he wanted to do something. He turned to Mr. Femm. 'Who's this fellow, Morgan? Your man? Is he as bad as all that? Couldn't you tackle him about it—tell him to get to bed?'

Mr. Femm, who did not look happy, shook his head. 'I have seen him once or twice like this before. Being little better than a brute, he is very close to Nature, and these upheavals have a bad effect upon him, and then he takes to drink and that makes him worse.'

'Could I tackle him?' Sir William looked masterful. 'I'm used to dealing with some pretty tough customers. He's the big rough chap I saw at the door here, isn't he?'

'He is. Very big, very rough, very strong.' A tiny smile crept into Mr. Femm's face. 'He is also dumb.'

'Dumb!' Sir William was taken aback. Somehow he couldn't see himself trying to reason with somebody who was dumb.

Mr. Femm nodded. 'Very strong, very stupid, and dumb. I said he was very close to Nature.' He nodded again and then walked away. Sir William stared and began to whistle soundlessly. This fellow was as odd as his servant. He joined the Wavertons at the fire.

CHAPTER VI

After they had all risen from the table, Gladys and Penderel found themselves standing together. There were several yards and the width of the table between them and the others, who were close to the fire. This isolation was accidental, but they were in no hurry to put an end to it. The mood of candour and revelation had passed, leaving them rather shy and awkward with one another, but something had been carried over from that shared feeling. Their faces were still strange but their feet were on common ground.

Gladys looked about her and gave a little shiver. 'Glad I'm not here alone,' she told him. 'This place'd give me the horrors.'

Penderel was curious. 'D'you mean absolutely alone?'

'No, I didn't really. I meant just with the people here.'

'The Femms?' He hoped that that was what she did mean.

She met his glance and nodded. 'Yes. There's something a bit queer about the man, but that little fat woman, with the voice—there's something about her ...' She finished the sentence by wrinkling her nose.

Penderel hadn't troubled himself much with the thought of Miss Femm. 'She's probably a harmless old creature, though she certainly does remind one of a slug.'

Gladys kept the wrinkle on her nose for a few moments more, then let it go and smiled. 'What's the time?'

He couldn't tell her. 'Sorry. No watch.'

'Fancy a man without a watch!' she cried, though the thought seemed to please her. 'But I never have one neither. Can't be bothered somehow. Why don't you?'

'I hardly ever want to know how it's going—the time, I mean; and if I do, there's always somebody ready to tell me. Some people never seem to think about anything else. I don't think I like watches and clocks. We ought to go back to hour-glasses and sundials, things that deal with time quietly and don't for ever pester you with their sixty seconds to the minute.'

She seemed to be looking at him rather than listening to him. 'You're a funny boy,' she said at last. 'I expect you've been told that before.'

Was this something real, only defeated by language, or was she becoming heavily arch? 'No, I haven't,' he replied lightly. 'I haven't been told anything for ages. I've been spending most of my time with men, and men, you know, never say things like that, never really tell you anything about yourself.'

'I can tell you something about myself,' she said, making a droll little grimace.

'What's that?' He put on a look of mock gravity.

She curved a hand round her mouth. 'I'm dying for a drink.'

'So am I,' he assented, heartily. 'This confessional business has made me thirstier than ever. Well, what about a drink? There's some gin left there.'

'Ugh! Not for me. I've not come to mopping straight gins yet. That'll be the last act. You wouldn't like to see me soaking gin now, would you?'

He admitted that he wouldn't. And he meant it. It was curious how the idea revolted him. He had a quick shuddering thought of gay and impudent youth, of something that deliciously held the balance between the urchin and the woman, rotted away: a mere trick, of course, of associations, but nevertheless very curious.

'Isn't there anything else?' she went on. 'One whisky now, and I'd face the rest of the night cheerfully. Sir Bill there, the greedy pig, swallowed all we had as soon as we came in. If you want to know how those men make so much money, that explains it. They're greedy pigs.'

Penderel looked at the table and rubbed his chin. 'I'm with you about the whisky. But there's none here.'

'Well, it's a damn shame, now, isn't it? Why don't you carry a flask?'

He stared at her and suddenly struck his left palm with his right hand. 'Why,' he cried, 'what a fool I am!'

'Of course you are.' She made a mocking little face. 'But what's the big idea?'

'I don't carry a flask as a rule, but I had one to-day. I'd forgotten all about it. You can hardly believe it, can you? But it's true. I had one, I had one, full of good whisky. I remember having one little drink out of it, when we started off again just after dinner.'

'What about it, then?' she asked him. 'You're not going to be a greedy pig, are you? You're not going to tell me now that little girls oughtn't to drink whisky?'

'Don't be silly. I'll go and get it and we'll share what there is, just the two of us.'

'That's the spirit.' Then her face seemed to change a little and now she really smiled at him. 'Just the two of us. We don't want Bill in this—he doesn't deserve any either—and the others won't want any. Where is it?'

'In my raincoat pocket, I suppose,' he replied. 'I'll go and see.' He went over to his coat, but returned shaking his head. 'It's not there. I must have left it in the car, somewhere on the seat.'

Her face fell. 'If that isn't just my luck. What's the good of having a flask out there? We can't start climbing over rocks and wading through rivers to find it.'

'But this car's here, just round the corner,' he said. 'You're forgetting that. I can easily slip out and get the flask.'

'Of course!' she cried. 'I was thinking of our car. Just a minute then, and I'll come to the door with you. I'll put my boots on first.'

'Have you got a torch?' he asked. When he discovered that she had, having carried Sir William's through the darkness, he continued: 'Well, if you let me have that, I can get the flask in a minute. No need for you to bother yourself, you know.' But he hoped she would.

When she returned, wearing her boots and coat and

carrying the torch, she said: 'No, I'll come to the door with you. It'll be something to do and perhaps we'd better have our drink there. I've shocked your friend—Mrs. What's-her-name—Waverton—enough for to-night. Besides, Bill will be wanting to butt in.' The others were clustered round the fire and were paying no attention to them. Gladys was eager to go, to do something. It would be a little adventure. She didn't want to stand there, waiting for him.

They left the big door open behind them and stood at the top of the three steps outside, sheltered from the rain by a small porch. The night was as black as ever and still roared gustily, and the light from behind only showed them a gleaming slant of rain and pools in the sodden gravel. For a minute or so they made neither movement nor sound but simply stood close together, looking out. Somehow it was as if all things had narrowed to one perilous rim.

'Give me London,' said Gladys, her mouth close to his ear. 'London every time. You never see a night like this there. It never seems so bad. Ugh! I'd get the horrors here. And, mind you, I've struck some rotten places in London, but you always feel you've only to make a little dash for it and everything's all right, there's the lights and the buses and policemen just outside. But look at this.'

'We're probably cut off altogether by this time.' Penderel found the idea attractive. The five of them were shipwrecked. There had come at last a break in the smooth and dreary sequence of things. He hoped they were cut off at least for a few hours. 'According to these people here, it's happened at least once before. The house itself is all right, but it might easily be impossible to get away from it.' But it didn't look impossible though, and he couldn't help wishing the evidence were plainer. He didn't want everything to settle down again.

Gladys surprised him by touching at once the core of his thought. 'You're rather pleased about it, aren't you? Anything for a bit of excitement's your motto, isn't it?'

'Perhaps it is,' he replied. 'But I hope you're not going on to say that you've met my sort before. That would make me very angry. I like to think I'm original.'

She reflected for a moment. 'No, I've met all sorts, and some were a bit like you but not really very like. You're different really.'

'Now that's a compliment,' he cried. 'Nothing like being different. You're different too.'

'Of course you'd have to say that, wouldn't you?' She turned her head to look him in the face. Her eyes seemed enormous in that strange half-light of the open door. 'But you don't really believe it. I know.'

'You don't know.' This was silly stuff, but he had an odd desire to tease her.

'Yes, I do. You shut up,' she retorted, quite calmly. 'Run away and get that flask. Where's the car?'

'Just round the corner here somewhere.' He waved his left hand. 'It's in a shed or coach-house or something and won't be locked up. Can I borrow the torch?'

She handed it to him. 'I'll wait here for you.'

'Right you are,' he cried. 'I shan't be long.' He hurried away, and a moment later she saw the light from his torch vanish behind a corner of the house. Three or four minutes passed for her in a kind of dream, in the very centre of which, far removed from the darkness and the rain, there seemed to be something comforting, warm, glowing. It would be fun when he came back with the flask. The drink didn't matter much—though she had missed the whiskies-and-sodas that most evenings brought, and felt a little uncomfortable, uncertain of herself—but she liked the idea of the two of them, just them and nobody else, sharing that flask, making a kind of cosiness together in the middle of this awful night. There was something about this boy . . . she felt she understood him. She had remembered him from that one night at the 'Rats and Mice.' He hadn't remembered her, hadn't noticed her. That was nothing. She wasn't so sorry about that. He had had a lot to drink, was nearly tight, but not red and goggly like most of

them, but pale, with very bright eyes, all strung up. He wasn't
the usual sort. He didn't care much about girls, but was one
of those who went round drinking with other fellows, played
cards for money all night, and talked and talked about the War
and books and politics and all that, very clever and very funny.
They'd think he was happy, they'd know no better; she could
almost see and hear them, a lot of men talking and laughing,
silly babies. That girl had done it for him, or begun it. She
found herself wondering what that girl was like. Tall and fair,
little head, high voice and snobby accent, cool sort of stare,
twenty-guinea tailor-mades as 'these old rags' for the morning
stroll, one kiss if you're a good boy—she'd be that kind, rather
like this one here he'd been staying with, Mrs. Waverton. But
he wasn't in love with this Mrs. Waverton, wasn't even interested, she could see that. Perhaps that girl wasn't the same
kind. And anyhow, what did it matter, what was she being so
silly about? It was time he was back.

Then something happened. The little lighted patch of
night, with its gleam of falling rain and wet ground, at which
she had been idly staring for the last five minutes, was suddenly
blotted out, and there was nothing but darkness before her.
The doorway was all dark. The lights in the house must have
gone out. It was all so sudden, so unexpected, so noiseless,
that for a moment or two she was completely bewildered and
rather frightened. Then she heard voices raised indoors. They
would be telling one another that the lights would have to be
attended to, that the fusing or whatever it was would have to
be put right. The lights would probably be on again in a few
minutes. She had said she would wait there. If she went in
now, she might spoil it all. She would stay where she was.

It was queer, frightening, though, standing there in the
dark and not knowing what was happening. She could at least
peep in, just to satisfy herself. There was a very faint firelight
creeping through the doorway now. She could hear voices
again, and footsteps, now a loud voice—that was the fat, deaf
woman, who must be quite close. She had been staring irres-

olutely at the darkened doorway, but now, having determined
to look into the house, she moved a pace or two forward and to
the right. Had she moved another step the heavy door would
have flung her back bodily, but as it was she stopped just in
time. Actually it did not touch her but it seemed to have been
banged in her face.

She was so startled that the crash left her dizzy, leaning
against the door for support. It was as if someone had dealt
her a blow. No gust of wind could have banged that great door
into its place; somebody inside had shut it; and she was locked
out. And now it was darker than ever, and all she could hear
was the noise of the rain, a dismal, frightening, lonely sort of
noise.

Why didn't he come back with that flask? Why didn't
somebody remember they were out and open the door? It had
only been shut by a silly accident. She would knock and let
them know she was there. But even when she made up her
mind, it seemed as if her muscles would not obey her at once,
so that she hesitated for some time, with one hand resting on
the door itself and the other ready clenched for the knocking.
She grew impatient with herself. What was the matter? A rap
or two would settle it. Yet when she did knock at last, it was
hurriedly and rather timidly, like somebody dubious of the
fate an opened door would bring. She waited a moment and
then knocked again, this time with more confidence.

Nothing happened. The massive door looked as if it were
closed for ever. The noise of the rain returned with greater
insistence, and the night, the immense black wet gulf of it,
seemed to close round her. What had happened in the house?
What had become of Penderel? She couldn't wait for him
any longer, everything had suddenly become so queer. If she
stood in front of that door another minute, she would want to
scream and batter it with her two fists. He didn't know these
things were happening, and he was only round the corner. She
would go and find him.

It was a relief to do something, even though it meant

splashing through the darkness. She made for that corner of the house round which Penderel's light had disappeared, but when she had groped her way to the other side of it there were no signs of any sheds or coach-houses. There was, however, some sort of light on the left, and she hurried towards it, imagining for a moment or so that she had found Penderel. But no, this was still the house itself. The light was shining through an uncurtained window on the ground floor. She went nearer and saw that the light came from a solitary candle and that someone was sitting in there. Could this be Penderel? No, it was not. She approached the window more cautiously now, and peeped in.

The candle was on a bare table and it showed her the figure of a man sprawling there, with a bottle of brandy and a glass before him. It was the huge dumb man she had seen when she first came in, the man they said was drinking, Morgan. She could not see him very distinctly because the window was streaming, but she received a vivid if fantastic impression of his humped shoulders and hairy flushed face. His head was rolling a little from side to side, and he put one great paw on the table to steady himself. He looked as if he had reached the brooding stage, and very soon, she thought, if he didn't fall asleep, he would turn nasty. She had seen them before—usually with two or three policemen hanging on to them before they had done—and he was obviously that sort and such a huge brute too. He would need about four policemen if he turned nasty. They ought to have locked him in that room, which seemed to be a kitchen. Perhaps they had, though. Now she saw him lift his head, and she felt a sudden stab of fear as he appeared to turn his eyes towards the window. But she reminded herself that he couldn't see her, and she stayed where she was, watching him, fascinated. Now he had rolled to his feet and was looking about him. He moved forward for a few paces and then stopped, swaying slightly and apparently muttering to himself. Obviously he hadn't reached the legless state as she thought he might have done, for he moved with some confidence, but he was drunk, there was no doubt about that, broodingly and dangerously drunk, ready for mischief and worse.

She turned away, dazed after looking at the light, and groped her way round the next corner, feeling wet and cold now and apprehensive. Where was Penderel? For a moment she was completely bewildered by the total darkness and splashed on helplessly, like someone lost and blind. But she heard a noise coming from the right somewhere. It sounded like a horse moving in its stable. She pressed on vaguely in the direction of the sound and seemed to approach a long black bulk. These must be the coach-house and sheds he had mentioned. Yes, there was a glimmer of light further away on the left. She hastened towards it, heedless of the pools through which she had to splash, and a moment later found herself blinking in the sudden full glare of the electric torch. She had found him.

'Is that you?' she called, halting.

'Hello!' came his voice, and she hurried forward. 'I was just coming back,' he went on. 'Sorry to have been such a time, but first I couldn't find the car and then I couldn't find the flask. I looked all round the back seat, then at last remembered I had passed it to Waverton and he had put it down and forgotten it, and it was on the front seat. Sorry to have kept you waiting.'

She was hardly listening. They were in a kind of shed, and she was at his side, leaning against him, breathless. She felt all weak now. 'Half a minute,' she gasped, and straightened herself.

He put a hand on her arm, and with the other hand sent the light of the torch circling round the shed. 'Hello, what's wrong?'

She waited a few moments. It didn't seem much now. He would think she was being silly. 'Nothing much really,' she told him. 'Only it seemed so funny. While I was standing at the door, waiting for you, all the lights in the house suddenly went out.'

'That's nothing,' he interrupted. 'They've been jumpy all the time. I've been expecting that. This home-made electricity's always going wrong, and a night like this just asks for it.'

'All right, Mr. Wise Man. I thought of that too. But there's some more. Just after the lights went out, the door was banged in my face. I was locked out.'

'That's queer certainly,' he admitted. 'Perhaps the wind though . . .'

'No, it wasn't. Then I knocked, but nobody came. I was fed up standing there, waiting for you, so I set off to find you, and on the way I saw that man Morgan in the kitchen, fighting drunk. Phew!' She blew out her breath. 'I want to sit down.'

'Of course you do,' he cried. 'You want a drink too. Well, then, inside or out?'

'What do you mean? If it's the drink, I want it inside.'

He turned her round and flashed the light forward. There was the car, which had been backed into the long shed. 'We can perch on the step or running-board or whatever they call it, or we can get inside and be snug and talk it all out over the whisky. Just a minute,' he added, moving forward. 'I'll switch on the lights to make it cosier. Only the dims though, because it's Waverton's electricity, not mine. There you are.'

'We'll sit inside,' she decided.

'Right you are. Front or back?' he enquired, bowing and waving a hand towards the two doors.

She laughed. He was turning it all into fun again. 'Oh, the back!' she cried. He held open the door and she climbed in and settled herself happily on the cushions. He sat down by her side and began to unscrew the flask.

'So they've shut us out, eh?' He was pouring the whisky into the little cup. 'Well, that's nothing new, is it? We're always being shut out.'

'I'm not.' She took the cup he offered.

He laughed. 'Aren't you? I am. Drink up, and then begin at the beginning and tell me all about it. Wait, though, I'll have a drink first. I don't suppose there's anything in it, I mean the business of the lights and the door, of course, but there might be, there's just a chance. If there were, it would be something horrible. Well, I drink your health, Gladys.' He drained the cup. 'I hope you don't mind my calling you that, as between fellow adventurers, you know, shut out, lost in the dark, draining the last flask.'

'No, I don't mind. I like it.' She felt warm now, snuggling in the seat and with the tiny fire of whisky somewhere inside her; and she found herself leaning against him a little, discovering a certain comfort in the suggestion of his neighbouring solidity. 'But what do you mean by your something horrible?' she went on to ask. 'Are you trying to frighten me?'

He was more serious now, though not entirely so. 'No, I'm not. I tell you I don't suppose there's anything in it. But, I repeat, if there were, it would be something horrible. What I mean is, that this house we've crept into out of the dark might be all right—that is, so far as we're concerned, just for to-night, we'll say—and probably will be, but it's very queer, and if it goes wrong, it'll go wrong very badly. I feel it in my bones. Once off the track and there'll be something hellish let loose. You see, I've been brooding over it a bit, and I know more about it than you do.'

'You're making it up,' she cried. 'You don't know any more than I do. You're trying to work it all up into something very exciting, just to pass the time. I know you.'

'Perhaps I am. But listen. To begin with, there's old Sir Roderick.'

'Who's he?'

'Exactly, who's he? You've never heard of him. But he's in there. He's the master of the house really and was once tremendously important, but is now very old and infirm and is somewhere upstairs, invisible and ungetatable. When you come to think of it, he's rather like God.'

She pinched his arm. 'You mustn't,' she told him, and meant it. It wouldn't do to say such things a night like this. He was worse than she was, and she would have to hold him in.

He didn't seem to resent the pinch and she let her hand stay where it was, loosely grasping his arm.

'Then there's woman Femm,' he continued. 'You've seen and heard her. She might break out anywhere. I'm not sure now she didn't frighten Margaret Waverton. There's Morgan. You've just seen him——'

'I have,' she broke in, with conviction, 'and I hope to God they've locked him in.'

'There's man Femm, those bones that have dodged the police. I wonder what he'd been doing, by the way. Now the queer thing about him is that he's terrified, absolutely jangling with fear of something or somebody in the house. I noticed it, and he said he was afraid of Morgan getting drunk——'

'If that's what it was, I don't blame him.' She was very emphatic.

'But it wasn't, that's the point. I'm positive it wasn't. It was something, somebody else. In the house too. Perhaps it's Sir Roderick, who may be a kind of old horror.'

She tightened her grip on his arm. 'That's enough of that. I want to be able to go back there.'

'All right. But you ought to have been telling your tale. Now you begin, and when you've finished, we'll go back and see what's really happened.' He sank a little lower in his seat and rested his head on the cushions. She began her story of the lights and the door, and as she spoke her head gradually slipped down until at last her cheek was resting against his sleeve. Throughout there was at the back of her mind the thought of that great closed door and the surrounding darkness and the rain that could still be faintly heard beating against the roof of the shed. But there was a little roof of their own, the car's hood just above their heads, between them and that other roof, and they seemed to be in a queer tiny room, smelling of leather and petrol, that lodged them warmly and securely in the very centre of the night, just the two of them, talking so easily together. She wanted to give herself a shivering little hug—just as she used to do when she was a kid and the curtain went up at the theatre—and she hadn't felt like that for a long time. It was queer how excited and happy she was inside, simply because the two of them were there talking about strange things and all the time talking their own strangeness away.

CHAPTER VII

It had looked as if Philip were going to plunge into an explanation, as if they were going to have it out together at last. They had drawn away from the others and were standing near the fire, intent upon one another. They ought to have begun as soon as that curious talk, which had pretended to be a mere game round the table, had come to an end. Indeed, their eyes had begun, Margaret told herself, and then admitted that it was mean of her to have left the actual cold plunge into talk to Philip. Poor Philip was so dreadfully handicapped. If he wasn't too proud to talk to her properly—and she was sure the night had withered away all but the merest husk of pride in both of them—he was still shy. Why had she stupidly waited and then squandered the precious moments in chatter. No, it wasn't really chatter, nothing they said now could be called that, but it wasn't the talk they wanted. Their eyes condemned it. Eyes were doing that everywhere, watching in despair the world being chattered away.

Then it had seemed as if he were about to begin. He had tightened his lips for a moment and that familiar little frown had appeared. How well she knew that look! There had been times too—and they weren't pleasant to think about now—when she had hated it, had turned away and had allowed other faces (Murrell smiling down at her, the sickly fool!—how could she have been so silly!) to come flashing into her mind. The little speech that had followed that look on his face had seemed to confirm her judgment. He had said, very gravely: 'Did you understand what I meant when I was talking at the table, Margaret? It was important, you know—I mean important for us.'

There was everything in that plural. Of course she had understood. As if she didn't know him, know every twist and turn of his mind, so anxious, blundering, honest, yes, gloriously honest! She had waited a moment before replying, but only to pick out the right words so that she could get the two of them really launched. And then, before she had spoken a word, it had happened. The lights had gone out. It was as if the house couldn't leave them alone. She was just finding her feet in it, that queer experience in that horrible room with Miss Femm was just beginning to look like a mere attack of nerves, everything was settling down into decency and friendliness, and now the light was gone. At first they seemed to be in total darkness, but it was soon partly dispelled by the dull glow from the fire. Now she stood among shadows in a faintly crimsoned cavern.

The fuss that followed was rather welcome; it did at least keep the house at bay. The men began shouting to one another about fusing and short circuiting and accumulators. Philip, who knew all about these things, offered to try and make the lights work again, but Mr. Femm seemed to think it was hopeless. Margaret didn't listen very carefully, being content that their loud, cheerful voices filled the darkness. But when Sir William struck a match and held it up and there was talk of candles, she remembered the one she had brought back with her from Miss Femm's room.

They lit this candle and put it on the table, and then they all drew a little closer and looked down on its tiny wavering flame. At this moment, Miss Femm marched in upon them, carrying another lighted candle.

'You've got one, have you,' she yelled at them. 'Well, look at it. It's guttering. There's a draught.' She looked round the room. 'The door's wide open.' She went over and closed it with a bang. Then she returned to the table, put down her candlestick, and let her little button eyes run from one to the other of them.

'Look here,' cried Sir William, heartily, 'isn't there anything else we could have, a lamp or something? Not much of a light this.'

'What's that?' Miss Femm screamed, looking at her brother. He explained in his curious hissing voice that always contrived to reach her ears. Meanwhile, Margaret seemed to hear a faint knocking, but as no one else appeared to hear it, she thought she must be mistaken. Then Miss Femm's voice drove all thought of it from her head. You couldn't think of anything else the moment that woman opened her mouth.

'Let them have the big lamp then,' she was saying. Miss Femm always talked about them to her brother as if they weren't there. 'There's oil in it. We used it the last time the lights went out. We must have some light down here, and not just to please them either. There's Morgan, remember. Go and get the big lamp, Horace. You know the one.'

He stared at her, his face an edge of bone in the candle-light. Then after a few moments' hesitation he stammered: 'Yes, I—I think so. I cannot remember where it is though. You get it, Rebecca.'

'Not I!' she cried. 'Too big for me. And if you don't know where it is, I'll tell you; though you know as well as I do. It's on the little table on the top landing.' Her voice rose to a scream of savage derision. 'You know where the top landing is, don't you? You've heard of it, I dare say. You can perhaps believe there's a top landing, even though you do believe so little. Well, it's up there, next to the roof.'

It was strange that Mr. Femm should seem so agitated. It wasn't the mere screaming that was upsetting him; he frowned his resentment at that; yet he was still hesitant and disturbed. 'I remember it now. Yes, the big lamp. It is very heavy, too heavy for me.' He shook his head. 'I couldn't carry it down all those stairs.'

'You mean you're afraid to go up there alone,' she screeched, pointing a finger at him. 'Well, I'm not going up, I've enough to do. You go with him.' And the finger was sharply turned until it pointed at Philip.

Margaret jumped and felt like crying out that Philip shouldn't go, but then suddenly realised she would be making a fool of herself. Why shouldn't he go? Yet she was half alarmed, half annoyed, when he nodded across at Mr. Femm. 'Yes, I'll go with you, of course, and help to get it down.'

'Get it myself, if you like,' Sir William put in, looking from one to the other.

Philip grinned at him. 'No; I've been chosen, and I'll go. We'd better have one of these candles, hadn't we?' He took up a candlestick, gave a smiling glance at Margaret, and moved a few paces forward. Mr. Femm joined him at the foot of the stairs, was given the candle, and then slowly led the way up. The others stared at them in silence, and it was not until both the men themselves and their jigging shadows had disappeared that anybody turned away or spoke.

'I want this,' cried Miss Femm, laying a hand on the remaining candle.

Margaret exclaimed in protest against being left in the dark for even a moment. Philip's queer little exit had somehow left her shaken, and now she regarded Miss Femm with positive hatred.

'Must leave us a light, you know,' Sir William shouted. And he gave Margaret a friendly glance, as if to suggest that he knew what she was feeling, a glance for which Margaret, who hadn't expected it, was instantly grateful. 'If you're going,' he went on, bellowing cheerfully, 'you must leave us this. Can't sit in the dark.'

In reply to this, Miss Femm, surprisingly enough, produced from the grey fat folds of her face a kind of smile. 'It would do you good to sit in the dark,' she told him, 'but I'll see. I can't go about in the dark and I'll have to find another for myself.' She fumbled in the bottom of the candlestick and found there an old candle-end, which she lit and held before her as she waddled away to the door that led into the corridor. The other two watched her for a moment and then settled themselves in front of the fire.

'I think I'll try a cigarette,' said Sir William, producing his case. 'Will you have one?'

She didn't really want to smoke, but she took one because it would help her to feel easy and companionable. Their being left alone together and the fire and the candle-light all combined to suggest, quite definitely if not strongly, a certain intimacy. You felt you ought to begin talking of something very personal and important almost at once.

Sir William blew out a column of smoke, leaned back in his chair, stretched out his legs, looked about him, and then remarked easily: 'Not very cheerful, is it? What's become of Gladys and that other chap, Penderel? Funny I never missed 'em. Are they wandering about the house somewhere?'

She replied that she wasn't sure. They might have gone out. He doesn't seem to be bothering much about his Gladys, she told herself. What a queer relationship! She felt suddenly curious about it, about him too, and stared across at his heavy face.

'We're a bit dictatorial with these people, when you come to think of it,' he mused. 'Don't know that I'd like it. Though we've every excuse, of course.'

'I know. If they were ordinary sort of people, I should say we were behaving very badly. But they're so queer, aren't they?' And then she suddenly thought how horrible it would be if he stared at her in surprise and blandly contradicted her. It would only need a touch like that, she felt, to throw her off her balance.

He only smiled, however, and there was comfort in his hearty rejoinder, for there seemed to be a whole sensible world behind it. 'A bit mad, I should say,' he replied. 'Both of 'em. They get like that, living in these places, miles from anywhere. Just imagine year after year, with many and many a night like this, and hardly seeing anybody. I know, because my own part of the world's a bit like this.'

She took the cigarette out of her mouth and looked her astonishment. 'Why, I see you against a background of telephones and cars and express trains and offices and factories. Nothing like this.'

'Now, yes. But not always. I came originally from a little
village in East Lancashire on the edge of the moors. A few
miles away from where I used to live it's as wild as this, and
you get some queer folk—people—up there.' She seemed to
hear the flat Lancashire accent creeping back into his voice. 'I
still go back sometimes. They tell me what they think of me
up there. I've a brother and sister there yet, living in the same
old way.'

She didn't know anything about these people, but she
remembered certain Scots novels. 'They don't make a fuss of
you, I suppose, because you're now an important person and
have made a lot of money?'

He laughed. 'Well, this is the way it works. They respect the
money but not me. They care about money up there, know
what it's worth, and don't pretend to despise it. Now in other
places, particularly in the South of England, they pretend
they don't care about money and they also pretend to think
a lot about me, who happen to have plenty. The other's the
best way, though I don't think so when I'm there and they're
putting me through it.'

Margaret couldn't resist it, he seemed so willing, almost
anxious, to be communicative. 'How did you come to make
such a lot of money? I mean, how did you begin?'

He looked across at her with thick, raised brows. 'That's a
queer question.'

'I'm sorry, it's rather a rude question, I know. But it's a question I've always wanted to ask someone like you.'

'Oh, I'm not offended, don't think that,' he cried, leaning
forward and then settling himself more comfortably in his
chair. 'It was queer because I happened to be thinking about
the very same thing.' He stopped and looked with half-closed
eyes at the fire. Margaret, released from her curiosity for a
moment, wondered what Philip was doing. He was a long
time returning from that mysterious top landing. But was
he though? No, he had only been gone a few minutes. She
returned with a rush to her companion, who had suddenly

lifted his head and was now looking across at her. 'Would you really like to know?' he enquired.

She nodded. 'Yes, I'm really curious.' If it was to be a tale of high finance, Philip would be back before it had hardly got under way. But she couldn't help feeling that it was going to be something more personal, for even in that dim light she seemed to recognise on his face that plunging look which men put on when they were about to unburden themselves.

'Unless you're very lucky,' he began, 'you only make money by wanting to make it, wanting hard all the time, not bothering about a lot of other things. And there's usually got to be something to start you off, to give you the first sharp kick. After you've got really started, brought off a few deals and begun to live in the atmosphere of big money, the game gets hold of you and you don't want any inducement to go on playing—d'you follow me? It's the first push that's so hard, when you're still going round with your cap in your hand. It's my experience there's always something keeps a man going through that, puts an edge on him and starts him cutting, and it may be some quite little thing. A man I knew, a Lancashire man too, was an easy-going youngster, thought more about cricket than his business, until one day, having to see the head of a firm, he was kept waiting two hours, sitting there in the general office with the clerks cocking an eye at him every ten minutes. He's told me this himself. "All right," he said to himself, "I'll show you." He walked out when the two hours were up, and that turned him, gave him an edge. He did show 'em, too. I don't say, of course, that every man who says something like that to himself brings it off, but some do. Well, it was the same with me.'

'What was it then that made you so ambitious?' And Margaret looked at him speculatively.

'It was a cotton frock,' he said quietly.

She stared and hastily smothered a laugh; obviously he was in grim earnest. He reminded her of a big brooding schoolboy. 'Tell me what happened,' she said softly.

'All right, I will, though I don't know why I should,' he remarked. Then he changed his tone. 'Just after I left school, I got a job in a cotton office in Manchester. I met a girl when I was twenty and very soon we were engaged. Couldn't get married for a year or two because I hadn't enough to do it on. At last they told me to leave my desk and start going on 'Change, in other words promoted me and gave me a good rise. That was enough for us, we got married. We hadn't much money, but what we had gave us a very good time. I was in love and very happy then. I wanted to do well at my job and kept my nose down to it during working hours, but forgot all about it at night and at the week-end. Still, I wanted to get on, and my wife encouraged me. Well, I was promoted again, this time to the London office, with more responsible work and another rise. We were excited about that, I can tell you. I can see us now, getting all our things packed—not that that took us long—ready for the great move. We found a little flat, very cheap, near Swiss Cottage, and Lucy—my wife—slaved away cleaning it up and I helped her when I came home at night, and we enjoyed ourselves I can tell you, though we'd no friends and nobody hardly spoke to us for months. But it was London and we felt we were getting on and we were happy together. We managed to spread the money out, and we'd have dinner in Soho once or twice a week and go to the theatre, in the pit. It was a bit lonely for her, but she didn't mind it at first. We'd soon find our feet, move up in fact. I bought a dress-suit, my first.' He stopped, stared at her, and cleared his throat. 'I don't suppose you want to hear all this. Don't know why I'm bothering you with it.'

'Go on, go on. I want to hear it,' she told him.

'Well, I'll make it as short as I can,' he went on. 'One of the directors gave a party, and we were invited. This was the great event. We felt everything was beginning for us. They were taking us up. You can just hear us talking it over, Lucy all nervous and excited, hoping to make a good impression for my sake. Well, I put on my dress-suit and she made herself as pretty as a picture. During the evening I didn't see much of her. I was among the men most of the time, talking business, making the most of the opportunity. Once or twice I looked across and gave her a smile and she smiled back, but I thought she looked a bit forlorn. I was full of it all going home, but she was very quiet, tired I thought. Then when we got to bed I pretended to go to sleep, but I heard her crying. When I asked her what was wrong, she said she was tired, got a headache. As a matter of fact she hadn't been feeling too well, so I left it at that. But I noticed she never mentioned that party. There was another a month or two afterwards, but she wouldn't go. She'd a good excuse then because by that time she was really ill. Within a year she was dead. But I found out what was the matter that night. She let it slip. She'd only had a cheap cotton frock on (it looked pretty enough to me, and I knew a bit about dress goods) and the other women there had let her know it. She was a little provincial nobody in a cotton frock and they didn't forget to let her see it. She'd had a wretched evening, had felt snubs and sneers in the air all the time. It kept coming out later, when she was weak, half delirious. I remember sitting by her bedside. . . .' He stopped and looked down into the fire.

Margaret waited, afraid of marching briskly into that reverie of his. At last she moved a little in her chair and he looked up. There was just light enough for her to see his face tightening.

'That did it for me,' he cried. 'Up to then I'd been the nice honest decent little servant of the Company. Well, that was finished. They couldn't give a poor little nobody in a cotton frock, all eyes and smiles and nervousness, a friendly word or look, couldn't they! I told myself I'd put them all in rags. I was mad, but it put an edge on me, strung me up as if I was a fiddle-string. Going home to that empty little flat night after night during the first year, I swore to myself I'd spend the rest of my life beggaring every woman who'd been to that party. Couldn't do it, of course, but I did what I could. Before I'd done, I took a lot of cotton away from some of those fellows and piled it

on the backs of their women. Within three years I'd wrecked
that company and walked over to its biggest competitor. That
started me. You wouldn't think I was sentimental, would you?
But that began it. And it wasn't hard because there was nothing
for me to do but to make money. I didn't even want to spend it
at first, nobody to spend it on, and didn't want to enjoy myself
or take it easy, not with that cotton frock stuck in my throat.'

He rose from his chair and kicked a log back into its place
on the fire. Then he stood looking down at her, his massive
face very clear in the candle-light.

'You'll hear some tales of me, probably heard 'em already.
I'm one of the rudest of the rude self-made men. I've no
respect for charming hostesses, nice ladies whose husbands
could do with a bit of capital, or dainty aristocratic girls
who wouldn't be above marrying a man twice their age if he
happened to have bought a title and owned a few factories and
ships and a newspaper. They'll tell you that, and they're right.
I keep my respect for the young men's wives who turn up in
cheap frocks. I suppose a man's got to be sentimental about
something, and that's how it takes me. I've slipped many a
year's dress allowance into an envelope. Queer, isn't it?'

Margaret murmured something, but she hardly knew what
it was, for she was troubled by a vision of factories and ships
and crowded offices, and against this background there stood
out the figure of this man, no, this huge resentful boy with
his oddly commonplace little romance, someone lost, now
smiling, now crying, in a tiny flat, one of thousands, nearly
thirty years ago. She stared at him. He had never really grown
up. Were they all like that, these men who grabbed power,
who wrecked whole countrysides, who sent other men flying
all over the world? Once again she seemed to ache beneath
the sudden pressure of life. It was time Philip returned. Why
didn't he come, bringing the lamp? She felt lost herself in this
queer light. The very look of that single candle, pointing at the
shadows, made her ache.

CHAPTER VIII

'What's that?' Sir William held up his hand. 'Didn't you hear something?'

Margaret leaned forward in her chair. 'I thought I heard a noise, a kind of distant rumbling.' She rose to her feet, and they stood together, listening. Their eyes were empty, but in their ears was the whole vague tumult of the night.

'Nothing much,' said Sir William at last. 'Storm's still going on, I suppose.' He thrust his hands into his pockets, and began whistling softly.

There had been so many things to think about that Margaret had almost forgotten the storm, the crumbling hills and the floods outside, the old menace of the night. Their journey through it, their arrival here, these events had crept away from the foreground of her mind, had thinned and faded a little. Now they returned, conquering her mind in one savage rush; the walls and the roof became mere eggshell; and the night was about to pour in its rain and darkness. She stood there pressing down so heavily upon one foot that the whole leg was taut and dully aching, and still she listened.

There was more distant rumbling, then at last a huge crash, coming from somewhere above and behind the house. 'I wonder what that was,' she said, looking at her companion.

'Something went then,' he exclaimed. 'More water coming down now, I suppose.' He went over to the window, rubbed it with his forefinger, and tried to peer through. 'Can't see a thing. It's as black as pitch.' He continued to stand there, with his face close to the window. 'I'll tell you what,' he said, after a minute had passed, 'I can hear something though. Sounds like rushing water, tons and tons of it. Come here and listen.'

She joined him at the window, which looked out at the back of the house. There was a noise of rushing water coming from

somewhere, not a loud noise yet very disturbing, suggesting
the presence of a gigantic hostile power. 'Is it coming down on
us?' she asked.

'All round us now, I should think,' he replied. 'Probably
finding its way in.'

Yes, the house was an eggshell perched on the hillside.
There was no security anywhere. This thought angered her;
she felt as if she had been cheated.

'It won't bother us,' Sir William was declaring. 'Only keep
us indoors here, and anyhow we don't want to go out.'

She hastened to agree, and told herself not to be so foolish.
A foot or two of water, a few tumbling rocks outside, a little
space of darkness, that was all, and what were they? The
trouble really was, she ought to be asleep, dreaming. There
came a fancy that it was the dreaming part of her, now awake
and active, that was taking hold of her experience, turning it
into queer stuff, flashing baleful lights upon it. They were now
both drifting away from the window, going back to the fire
again.

The opening of a door behind turned them round. Could
it be Philip at last? No, it was Miss Femm. She came in with a
candle in one hand and with the other outstretched, a finger
pointing at Margaret.

'You opened it, didn't you?' she screamed, accusingly. 'Well,
you can go and shut it now, go and shut it. I can't. No time
to lose either. It's down on us, coming in too, I expect, in the
cellars.'

Margaret couldn't find a word. She felt rather sick. Sir
William, however, took charge of the situation. 'What's this?'
he called, with some sternness.

'The floods, of course!' cried Miss Femm. 'All round us.'

'Yes, I know that,' he returned. 'But what's this about
opening and shutting?'

'My window.' She pointed to Margaret again. 'She must
have opened it, and now she can shut it. I'm being swamped
out.'

Margaret found her voice. 'I'm sorry.' Then she turned to Sir William and lowered her voice. 'I'm afraid I opened the window in her room. That's what she means.'

'Is that all? Well, I'll go and close it for her,' he replied, to her relief. 'All right,' he shouted, nodding to Miss Femm. 'I'll come and shut it.'

Miss Femm nodded in reply, keeping her mouth tightly closed and fixing her little eyes on Margaret in a long evil stare. Then she went over to the door through which she had just entered, the one that led into the corridor that Margaret knew, and held it open. Sir William walked towards it, then turned and looked back at Margaret. 'Shan't be long,' he told her. 'Your husband ought to be back with that lamp in a minute or two.' He went out, followed by Miss Femm, who banged the door behind her.

It was a desolate sound. Nor was the silence that came so swiftly afterwards any more comforting. There dripped into it the thought that she was now alone. The shadows, thick in every corner of the big room, lit so feebly, despairingly, by the solitary candle, crept nearer to tell her that she was alone. It was only for a minute or so, though. Any moment might bring Philip down those stairs. She walked slowly over to the foot of the staircase and stood there looking up into the gloom above and listening for his footstep. She heard something, a vague noise, it might have been someone talking or moving about upstairs. Was it Philip and Mr. Femm? And if not, who was it, and what had become of them? There was a creaking somewhere. Was it on the stairs above? She glanced round the hall and then had a sudden impulse to run upstairs and find Philip. It would be better than staying there alone. But would it? She might miss him; he might return some other way, down another staircase at the back, and find her gone; and she might be wandering about upstairs. Who knew how big and rambling the house might be! She saw herself creeping down strange dim corridors. No, she would remain where she was. And anyhow, Sir William would return soon.

She wandered back to the table and looked down on the candle-flame. Idly she held one hand above it and began twiddling her fingers, watching their play of light and shade. Then she saw the shadows they cast, a dance of uncouth crazy figures, savages leaping in the smoke of a ceremonial fire, and she brought her hand away and remained quite still for a few moments, feeling very small and desolate. Soon she grew impatient, first with herself and then with everybody else. Why had they all stolen away, leaving her alone? Her mind swayed towards unreason. There came gibbering into it the fancy that she was the victim of a plot, that all the others had been deliberately spirited away by Miss Femm, who would lock them all up and then come creeping back to lay a toad-like witch's hand upon her. For one sickening moment she could feel that hand, but the next instant the whole fantastic web was broken. Nerves and a too eager imagination were playing her false again, playing false indeed to life itself, through which there ran the unbroken cord of sanity; they were lying and treacherous, betraying her mind back into primitive darkness. You go native, they whispered, it's easier. Thought came to steady her, and things shifted back into a reasonable shape and colouring again.

She was ridiculously impatient, of course, she told herself, swelling every second into a minute, but still it was queer how long everybody seemed to stay away. And where were Penderel and that girl Gladys? They must be together, of course. Perhaps they had tucked themselves away in some corner of the house (somehow the idea made her shudder), or they might possibly be outside.

The thought steered her towards the door. She would have a look at the night. Even if no one had returned by the time she came back from the door—and that was improbable—a peep outside would at least make things easier by contrast, would banish the desolation of the room, give it a suggestion of warmth and security. She opened the door and peered out. At first there was nothing but darkness and a rush of sweet cold air in her face. Then the light of the room, dim as it was, stole through and her eyes began to sift the dark. There were still noises coming from a distance, the sounds she had heard before, but these only formed a vague tumultuous background for other and more curious sounds, near at hand, all watery sounds, a kind of mixed lapping and swishing and splashing. She leaned forward and looked more closely. There was little or no rain now, only a few drops came spattering in the rising wind. But what was that faint curved gleam below? She peered down and saw that two of the three steps from the door had disappeared. Then she understood, though it was difficult to say how much her eyes actually saw. But that was water that darkly shone and lapped and swished and splashed there below. She was looking out upon what was virtually a river or a lake. The flood had come pouring down upon them, had rolled round the house (and was perhaps filling the cellars this very minute), and its waters had risen to a sufficient height to cover the two steps. It was besieging them. She was standing on the edge of a little island. Involuntarily she drew back and swung the door a little further forward, but did not close it. Fascinated, half lost in a dream, she still stared out, her fancy deepening the dark water every moment until she brooded over whole drowned valleys.

Then suddenly she went cold and stiffened. Somebody was standing behind her, very close. For a moment or so she did not move and there came back to her, in one crazy flash, that vision of Miss Femm which tormented her before. It was she who was standing there, malignant, corrupt, a witch.

There was a shuffling movement and the sound of heavy breathing. She had no need to turn and look now. It wasn't Miss Femm, it was Morgan. A great hand came uncertainly over her head, touched the door she held, and began closing it; she could feel his hot breath; he was brushing against her; there came a sickening animal warmth, a rank smell.

One quick desperate twitch of her whole body and she was free. The door crashed to, with all his weight upon it, and for a moment he remained there, leaning against it, a breathing hulk. She stood trembling, only a yard away, and stared at him. She wanted to cry out, but she dug her nails into her palms and remained silent, asking herself frantic questions. He was drunk, of course, as they said he would be. Had he been simply trying to shut the door? Yes, that was all. She had only to keep quiet, to be calm, dignified, and he would be gone in a minute.

Without another glance at him, she walked slowly across the hall towards the fire. It was extraordinary how far it seemed. Her back crept with little shivers. But it was all right; he would go away, and somebody would be coming soon, yes, somebody would be coming. She had reached the table now and the candle burning there gave her confidence. What was he doing? She turned to see, narrowing her eyes. The dim light showed him to her still standing there, a vague shape at first, but then she saw that he was no longer leaning against the door but had turned round to face her. Was he looking at her? The blur of his face told her nothing, but she felt sure that he was staring across at her. It would have been less terrifying if she could have seen him clearly, but that vague mass, that dark hulking shapelessness, like something monstrous spawned by the shadows, appalled her. Was he moving forward or merely swaying? And there was not a sound; nobody was coming. The whole world was suddenly empty and horrible.

Yes, he was coming towards her, there could be no mistake about that now. She saw him lurching forward gigantically. She wanted to run away. But he had stopped again, and was swaying there not two or three yards from the table; and she could see him clearly now, could see his hair and dripping beard and even his little sunken eyes, and this was something for faint comfort, for he did at least become a person again. Desperately she told herself it was only Morgan, the servant here, a big stupid creature. Why should she stand looking at him like that? If she took no notice of him, he would probably go away. She turned a shivering back upon him and walked slowly across to the other side of the fireplace. Then she faced about sharply. He too had moved and was now standing where she had been a moment before.

'What do you want?' she cried shakily. Her voice sounded so feeble that it only emphasised her weakness, her loneliness. And what was the use? He was dumb. If only he hadn't been dumb, she felt, she could have done something with him.

His little eyes dwelt upon her, as if in answer to her question. Then he raised a hand lumberingly and his mouth seemed to gape into a grin.

She held herself tightly. 'Go away,' she cried again, and stared at him. He did not move but made an uncouth noise in his throat. There came with it that smell again, rank from a huge unwashed hairy body. If he could only say something, however foul, it would have helped her to control herself. But this sickened and terrified her. Still trying to look self-possessed, she moved away again, with wincing little steps, this time round the right-hand side of the table, thus keeping it between them. She would go towards the stairs. Philip was up there somewhere and might be coming down any moment.

She could see Morgan out of the corner of her eye. He was still standing there, watching her. Now she was turning away from him, facing the bottom of the stairs. There was a noise behind her. Had he moved? She quickened her pace and was now within a yard of the lowest stair. He was following her; he was very near. Then she gave a little shriek for a hand fell upon her shoulder, twisting her round. A great arm swept about her, and there was a fleeting nightmare of a lowered hairy face, a suffocating hug, heat and stench and huge sliding paws. She threw herself back, struggling wildly, sickeningly, beating upon the arm that held her, wriggling desperately in his grasp. A sharp tearing—the top of her dress ripped—and she was free, stumbling backward, gasping. He loomed above her, but now she summoned all her strength, darted blindly beneath the outstretched arm, and contrived to scramble up the first few stairs.

'Philip, Philip!' she called with what breath remained to her.

Oh, where was he, where was he? The stairs heaved and trembled; her hair fell in front of her eyes, which saw strange flashes of light; there was a roaring in her ears; but he was coming after her now and she clutched at the banisters and pulled herself up and up, half falling and then recovering herself at every other step. He was there grunting behind her, only a few feet away. The stairs now curved into darkness, and in a moment she would be at the top. Something freed her voice at last, breathless though she was. 'Philip, Philip!' she called, and now the cry went ringing through the dark. 'Philip!' it went ringing again, sending her terror and her need clamouring through the upper rooms and landings, the black space into which he had disappeared. He was there somewhere and he would hear.

CHAPTER IX

Following Femm upstairs left ample time for reflection. He seemed to move not merely slowly but with downright reluctance, as if he were climbing to the scaffold. Philip was telling himself that he felt a durned sight better. He had Penderel (and the house itself too, perhaps) to thank for that, because it was that outburst of confidences round the table that had done him good. To begin with, he had let off steam himself, which made an immense difference. Then Margaret's answer to his question had told him a great deal. In fact, he had thought of trying to put things right between them, had just been about to begin—led on by the good old Come-now-Philip look in Margaret's clear eyes—when the confounded lights went out and eyes and all disappeared. Then, too, the others had rushed in to give themselves away, and that had been a warming and heartening kind of experience. The night had redeemed itself. If you can put yourself right with people, he announced to himself, the rest doesn't matter; the roof can fall in. And a serious young architect couldn't put it stronger than that.

So far he had been climbing funereally in Femm's shadow. Now they had reached the top of the first flight of stairs, and his guide had come to a halt and was holding the candle above his head, as if he were inviting the architect in Philip to look round. There wasn't much to be seen, but Philip peered curiously and suddenly found himself interested. He turned to examine the panelling at his elbow, and Femm brought the light nearer.

'Seventeenth century?' Philip asked.

'That was when this house was built, or at least some of it,' Mr. Femm replied, and seemed anxious to remain where he was and to volunteer further information.

Philip nodded to all that was said, looked about, touched

things. Everything there was magnificently done but had been wickedly neglected and was now in a ruinous state of decay; it was a sight that went to his heart. He thought he understood now why the house had depressed him at first, where he had picked up the idea of an evil desolation, for everything told the same sad tale, and no doubt downstairs he had quite unconsciously taken in all this. Treated with anything like decency, this house would have been a joy, a miracle. Now they stood there holding a candle to a fallen empire of craftsmanship. A not unpleasant melancholy, touched with autumnal beauty, invaded his mind. He wanted to talk about it to somebody, to Margaret.

They moved slowly down the landing, past several stout old doors. The last of these Mr. Femm tapped with his forefinger. 'This is my room,' he said, halting. 'There are some things here that you would like to see, I imagine.' He looked at Philip almost wistfully.

'I've no doubt I should,' Philip replied, 'but not just now, if you don't mind. We've got to get that lamp, you know.'

Mr. Femm lowered the candle and then made use of his other hand to stroke his long chin. He looked most fantastically bloodless, brittle. 'Ah, yes, the lamp.' He stared at Philip for a moment, then pushed his face forward a little. 'Why should we bother about the lamp? We have been long enough away now. We can go back and say that we cannot find it or that it was too heavy for us or that it is broken. They will have to believe us. Why should we trouble about the lamp?' He spoke very softly but with even more precision than usual.

Philip looked at him in amazement. What was the matter with the man? 'I don't see the point,' he began, then broke off and changed his tone, feeling rather indignant. 'Besides, we couldn't do that. We said we'd get the lamp and we'll get it. Why shouldn't we?'

'Why should we if we don't want to?' said Mr. Femm, calmly. 'And I don't want to. Are you afraid of telling a few lies? If you are, I will take it upon myself to tell them.'

'It's not that, though I must say I don't like lying. And in this case it would be particularly mean.' But Philip couldn't be angry, it was all so absurd. He never remembered a more absurd conversation—the two of them standing there in the little glow of candle-light at the end of the landing, arguing about a tiny errand they had undertaken.

'I must say, if I may do so without offence,' Mr. Femm mused, 'that for a man of culture, as you have just proved yourself to be, you are singularly naïve. Perhaps you have religious convictions, like my sister. Perhaps God is on your side.'

'No, I've not,' Philip replied shortly. He was beginning to be annoyed. There was something offensive about the man, a queer unpleasant streak in him that could hardly be dismissed as eccentricity. But something came to break his thought. 'Hello, did you hear that?' he exclaimed. It was a stifled cry from somewhere, and there came with it a kind of battering noise.

The candle dipped and shook, and in its wavering light Mr. Femm, who had started back, looked more ghostly than ever. He answered Philip's stare with hollow eyes. 'I did hear something,' he said at last.

'I should think you did,' Philip returned. It was rude, but he couldn't help it. 'What was it?' he demanded bluntly.

The other leaned forward again. 'It must have been Morgan. That fellow is drunk, as you know. He is probably making a disturbance in the kitchen.'

The sound had not come from the direction of the kitchen, but Philip couldn't very well pursue the topic, although his mind had not dismissed it. They were wasting time. 'Well, what about the lamp?'

Mr. Femm bit his lip and then looked apologetic. 'Listen,' he began, 'I want you to excuse me from accompanying you. I am tired and I am not strong. I cannot face any more stairs. I should have told you before, but vanity—the vanity of age— would not allow me. You know where it is, I believe. You will find it on a small table nearly at the end of the next landing above'—he pointed—'at the top of the stairs there.'

The man was so obviously lying that Philip could have laughed in his face. His excuses were sheer impudence. There was something very strange in all this, but there was nothing to be done about it. 'All right. I see,' he said, looking him steadily in the eyes. 'I'll go and get it. I suppose,' he added, remembering his companion's objection downstairs, 'it's not too heavy for me to carry?'

'Not at all,' came the reply. So that had been a lie too. The man was made up of them. What an extraordinary shifty, spectral creature he was! That's what's the matter with him, why I haven't liked him from the first, Philip told himself: he's a born liar himself and he makes everything, yes, the whole world, seem hollow and false.

'I shall want that, you know.' And Philip held out his hand for the candle. Mr. Femm begged him to wait a moment and disappeared into his room. When he returned he was carrying a burning night-light and, without a word, he now handed over the candle and remained standing at his door while Philip hurried forward to the foot of the next staircase.

He was not half-way up when he heard the sound of a door closing behind him. Evidently Mr. Femm had retired into his room. And the next moment there came the sound of a door either being bolted or locked. It seemed as if Mr. Femm were determined to feel secure. It was all very strange, and Philip stopped to tell himself so and to listen again. Somehow he didn't like the sound of that door. It was odd how a little thing like that could leave you feeling uncomfortably insecure yourself, almost as if you were left naked. He went on, but now he trod very lightly on the stairs. They were narrower than those below, uncarpeted and given to creaking long after your feet had passed over them. In the moving glimmer of candle-light everything here looked very uncared for and melancholy. Above his head was a little black skylight where the rain went rap-rapping. It was a place of dust and mildew and long decay, of things forgotten by the sunlight, as strangely remote as some house, fragmentary, shadowy, in the dark of a dream.

Here was the landing before him, and there, nearly at the end of it, were the little table and the lamp. To examine them coolly was to disperse the fairy-tale dusk that had somehow gathered in his mind as this absurd little errand had lengthened out and become touched with fantasy. The lamp was one of those old-fashioned double-branched affairs, its twin glass cylinders covered with dust. With care, he ought to be able to carry it down in one hand. The light of his candle fell on an old steel engraving hanging above the table, and it showed him a bewhiskered officer standing, sword in hand, in front of a large cannon, while in the background there towered a quite impossible pagoda. For a moment he stopped to gaze at this unknown, evidently a hero of one of the old Chinese wars, and to wonder how he came to be there, with his sword and his cannon and his pagoda. Then he took up the lamp, held out the candle at arm's length, and returned, more slowly and carefully now, along the landing.

He had been in such a hurry to discover the table and the lamp that he had never noticed that door on the left. Now, as he walked slowly back, it invited his attention, then arrested it. There was nothing very odd about its appearance; it was merely a stout old door that had lost most of its paint; but there was something very odd about the way in which it was closed. Then he saw what it was. The door had two large bolts. It was fastened on the outside. Why should they have done that? Did they suppose someone would break into the house that way? The very idea of anyone breaking into this house was monstrous. Pondering these things, he had actually passed the door, when something pulled him up. He seemed to hear somebody moving about. Surely there was the sound of a voice too, a kind of muttering not very far away? It could only come from behind that door. There was somebody inside that room, the thickness of a wall away from him, behind that bolted door. And what about that stifled cry he had heard a few minutes ago, that battering noise? Curiosity, like a little flame in the mind, burned and brightened for a moment and then suddenly went out, leaving him in a crawling darkness, with doubt and terror. He felt suddenly sick and terrified of life.

Yet he had not halted a minute when his ears seemed to catch another cry, this time from below, out of another world. Margaret. Surely that was her voice calling his name? Or was it that old trick of memory, a phantom call? There was silence now and he moved forward, but doubtfully. No, there was no mistake. 'Philip, Philip!' All of her in the cry, and a terrible urgency. Still mechanically clutching at the lamp, with neither hand free to balance himself, he rushed down the stairs, miraculously without falling; and immediately that feeling of mental sickness and terror vanished and a curious kind of anger stirred in him. He'd left her confident and smiling, and now even she'd been dragged into it. It couldn't leave even her alone. His mind, outracing him, found an opposing presence, an enemy, but no name for it; a density of evil, something gigantic, ancient but enduring, only dimly felt before, but now taking the mind by storm; it was working everywhere, in the mirk of rain outside, here in the rotting corners, and without end, in the black between the stars. Margaret never seemed to understand about it, but now it had made her understand or she wouldn't be calling like that. He'd been telling himself it was high time she did understand, but as he hurried on now to find her, the thought that it had got at her while she had been waiting, smiling there, below, roused him to fury.

As soon as he reached the lower landing, he hastily set down the lamp and ran forward. There was a flash of blue, a flying fair head, and she was clinging to him, her hands grasping the lapels of his coat. She was battling for breath. 'Morgan— drunk—got hold of me—coming now' was all that he could catch, but it was enough. The next moment the man himself, incredibly hulking in that light, had appeared, but he stopped short, a few yards away, when he saw the candle and the two of them standing there.

Margaret swiftly turned her head, then tugged at his coat. 'He's there. Let's get away from him.'

Philip shook his head, gave a quick glance round, then fixed his eyes on Morgan's dark bulk. 'There's a doorway just behind us,' he told Margaret. 'If he comes on, get behind me and stay in the doorway. There'll be plenty of time to run afterwards, if it's necessary.'

'Let's go, Philip. I'm terrified of him.'

He watched Morgan steadily. The man was swaying a little, but otherwise he made no movement. 'He's probably drunk himself silly and is only wandering about aimlessly. Are you sure he was after you?'

'He followed me round downstairs,' she whispered fiercely. 'I was all alone. Then he caught hold of me, and when I escaped he followed me up the stairs.' He could feel her trembling. 'Let's go now. We might find the others.'

'I don't know where they are.'

What was Morgan going to do? Philip watched him with anxiety, for the fellow was obviously as strong as a gorilla and was probably half-crazy, and Philip, though he was fairly tough and was at least sober, was by no means confident that he could stand up to the brute, let alone overpower him. He didn't even know what exactly he would do if Morgan advanced. He hadn't used his hands on a man for years, though there was a time when he had known how to box. Nevertheless, he was determined not to turn his back on the man, not to budge. The anger that had been so curiously fired in him on the way down still remained. Whatever the man may have done already, he still seemed a mere foolish lump; but if he changed to anything worse, Philip would oppose him whatever it cost. And anyhow Margaret could easily escape, could run downstairs—not upstairs, to that landing above, to that room.

'If he comes on,' he whispered, 'and you want to escape, slip past and run downstairs. Don't forget.'

Her eyes met his for a second. 'I shall stay here,' she said very quietly. She was composed now. 'Let me have the candle.' And she took it from him, moving a little to one side.

Morgan shuffled his feet and then suddenly lurched forward.

'Stay where you are,' Philip called sharply. 'What do you want?'

He contrived to pull himself up. Then his great shaggy head came forward and they could see his eyes, fixed in a stare. As if in reply to Philip's question, he made a gobbling noise in his throat and slowly raised a hand until it pointed at Margaret.

There was something overpowering in the very tongueless bulk of the man, and his approach had shaken Philip at first, sending a flash of fear through all his nerves. Run, run, run, they screamed. But this amazing gesture, this raised and pointed hand, so angered him that his nerves were immediately mastered. He extended an arm and gently pushed Margaret so that she stepped back into the doorway behind him. The light she held fell on Morgan, but left Philip shadowy. He watched those little glassy eyes, now turned from Margaret to him; and leaning forward slightly, balancing himself upon his toes, he waited.

Nor had he long to wait. Something flared up at last in Morgan's dull brain. Suddenly his arms pawed the air and he hurled himself upon Philip. This blind rush was Philip's opportunity and he leaped to take it, throwing all his weight behind one straight hard punch. Crack!—it went home, full in that lowered rushing face. Philip recovered himself and instantly stepped back, to be out of reach of those great arms. But for the moment he was in no danger. Only his sheer bulk had saved Morgan from being felled by the blow, which had been well-timed and had found his jaw; and even as it was he was sent reeling back. Philip did not follow up his advantage but remained where he was, at once bewildered and exultant, on the defensive. Perhaps that punch (undoubtedly a whacker) had knocked some sense into the brute, who had finished staggering back and was now gropingly bringing his hands to his head. He felt Margaret's hand on his sleeve and turned to smile at her. She was standing pressed back into the doorway, and in the light of the candle she was holding she looked very pale and shining-eyed. A noise in front brought him sharply round again. And he was only just in time.

Morgan had charged like a bull and was upon him. He had just time to raise his arms and tighten his body when the man's whole weight was flung upon him and he found his arms gripped by those huge hands. All was lost. Instinctively, however, he immediately twisted his arms so that his hands clutched at Morgan's coat sleeves, then he held on tightly, his arms rigid, and instead of trying to withstand the charging weight of his opponent, slackened his whole body. The result was that he did not go down but was rushed backward, past Margaret and down the landing, just as if Morgan were carrying him. It was a dreadful sensation, this of flying help-lessly backward, but he contrived to keep his wits. So long as he was not actually borne down, with Morgan's weight upon him, so long as one of those hands had not found its way to his throat, it might be still possible to master this brute, who seemed as gigantic but as brainless as a prehistoric monster.

He had found his feet again. This was the moment. He relaxed his grip for a second, brought his arms down and then threw them upward and outward with all his strength. Morgan was not quick enough to retain his grip and Philip was free to throw himself backward. He went further than he intended, crashing against the wall, because as he moved a blind swing of Morgan's clenched hand, as big as a mallet, caught him on the side of the head, nearly turning him sick. But the light was very dim here and Morgan's own bulk now blotted out most of it. He didn't seem to know exactly where Philip was, and when he charged again, he moved straight forward. Philip threw out a leg and, as Morgan went flying over it, summoned all the strength left to him and aimed a savage swinging blow at the man's body, a blow that landed somewhere in the ribs and completed his destruction. There was a great thud and with it the sharper crash of broken glass.

Morgan was there, measuring his length on the ground, and in his fall he had smashed the lamp that Philip had put down not so many minutes before. That was the end of the lamp then; and the end too, he hoped, for a time of Morgan, now a dark unstirring shape.

Philip leaned against the wall, triumphant but dizzy and sick. For a moment he did not move, but then tried a few faltering steps towards the light. His head ached and this narrow place couldn't contain the loud beating of his heart. Once more he leaned against the wall, and now he closed his eyes, desiring nothing but to be a breath in the darkness. But the light, coming nearer, forced his eyes open again. It was Margaret. Her arm was about his neck, her cheek pressed against his, and there came back to him, bringing a multitude of flashing little images from a life long lost, the scent of her hair. 'It's me, Phil,' she was saying. He remembered that, too. It had come back with the rest, across a desert.

Her fingers were moving gently across his face. 'Are you hurt?'

He opened his eyes very wide now and shook his head. 'No, at least nothing much. Just one bang. I was very lucky though.' He smiled at her and then looked down at Morgan, who was still lying there, motionless.

She followed his glance. 'He's not—not dead, is he?'

He took the candle from her. 'No fear. Probably hardly stunned. He went down with a fearful whack, but he's obviously a tough subject and there's probably nothing wrong with him. Let's have a look at him.' He held the light above the outstretched Morgan, who was stirring a little now and breathing heavily, and Margaret came peeping over his shoulder. 'He's only knocked himself out,' Philip told her. 'He'll be conscious again in a minute unless he happens to fall asleep; and it's more than likely that he will fall asleep, because he's very drunk.'

Margaret raised her eyes dubiously to his. 'Suppose he—begins again?'

'He won't. Don't worry about that.' Philip took her arm and began moving away. 'When he comes to his senses he won't remember anything, and he probably won't be fit for much, anyhow.'

Margaret tightened her arm against his fingers. 'I can't imagine how you did it, Phil.'

He laughed. 'That's obviously the right remark and just the right tone of voice, my dear. You caught the note of pride. Well, I can't help feeling rather like Jack-the-Giant-Killer. And, as a matter of fact, I can't imagine how I did it either.'

They were walking slowly back along the landing now. Suddenly Margaret stopped. 'Listen, Phil. You see that room there, the door where I was standing?'

'Yes.' What was this? The dark house closed round him again.

'There's someone in there, a man I think. When I was standing there I heard him call out, in a tiny weak voice.'

'Femm's in one of those rooms,' he told her. 'He left me and carefully locked himself in. But it's the one behind, not this one.' His mind was back on the landing above now, before that other door; it seemed a place in a nightmare. Should he tell Margaret about it? No; at least not yet.

'I distinctly heard somebody. He seemed to want something. It must be that other one.'

'What other one?' He had forgotten who was here, feeling lost for the moment in a maze of dream-like corridors that offered nothing but mysterious doors and voices crying in the dark.

'The oldest, the one they called the master of the house, Sir Roderick,' Margaret whispered. 'Don't you remember, they said he was very old and ill? I'm sure he wanted something. And think of him lying there, hearing all that noise, quite helpless perhaps.'

Yes, this must be old Sir Roderick, whose house had given them shelter. And what a house, what shelter! He looked at Margaret doubtfully, and then at the door itself. They were standing in front of it now, and its rubbed panels shone a little in the candle-light.

'Listen!' And Margaret's hand went up as she leaned forward, her white shoulder curving through the blue silk where her dress had been torn, her head a medallion of bright gold. His heart went out to her as he listened. She turned her head, her eyes seeking his. 'Did you hear that?' she whispered.

He nodded, then raised his brows in an unspoken question. There had come to them, as if from across a great space, the sound of a voice calling within, the tiny weak voice that Margaret had described. He read her decision in her face, and felt no surprise when he saw her hand creep forward to the door and tap-tap upon it gently. Her other hand sought his arm and rested there.

'Come in.' Their ears caught it as their eyes might have picked out a point of light on a midnight sea.

Margaret hesitated, and Philip felt her hand squeezing his arm. He put the candle into her other hand, leaned forward and slowly opened the door. His shadow went wobbling into the room, he went after it, and Margaret followed him.

CHAPTER X

They were still sitting snugly in the back of the car, and now the talk had drifted round to Sir William Porterhouse. Gladys was determined to explain about him, rather to Penderel's alarm, though he admitted to himself that he felt curious.

'Of course I like him,' she was saying, 'or I wouldn't go away with him. You can depend on that. But I'm just about as much in love with him as I am with old Banks, the doorkeeper at the Alsatia. I'm not going to put on any airs with you—we're through with anything like that, aren't we? And that's funny too, when you think we've only just met.'

'Yes, but we met in the middle of a black night,' he told her. 'And that makes the difference. It's too damned lonely putting on airs a night like this. And then there isn't much time.'

'How d'you mean, there isn't much time? There's plenty of time. There always is.' But she was hurt rather than puzzled. He must mean that he wouldn't be seeing her any more after this, and somehow she had expected he would be, quite a lot.

'I don't know what I meant,' he said. And he didn't, now that he came to think of it. It was just a queer spurt of emotion, feeling all things rushing by them. 'I think I must have meant the usual poetical Preacher stuff: we're like flowers that are fresh in the morning and withered in the evening; you must know the sort of thing.'

'Oh, that!' She dismissed these antique fancies with hearty contempt, all the more hearty because she felt suddenly relieved. 'That's only true about looks, when you're bothering about your face and figure. But it's not true about anything else, is it? Everybody I've ever met had more time than they knew what to do with; even old Bill there—with all his cables and telegrams and private secretaries and rushing about—has more gaps than he knows how to fill; I know that. Those old fellows—they read 'em out in church, don't they?—must have really been Beauty specialists.'

'Perhaps they were—in a way,' he put in, reflectively. 'But what were you going to say, before you began about not putting on any airs?'

'Oh, yes. About me and Bill. Well, it really boils down to this. It's been a convenient arrangement for both of us. As I said before, I like him, and he's helped me a lot, given me a pretty good time. There's been nothing regular about it, you know; no little flats and all the rest of it; he's just taken me out when he's felt like it or when I've felt like it, and we've had a few week-ends away. This is the longest and the farthest: I was down on this one from the start, but he was desperately keen, wanted a day's golf at Harlech. If he was like some of them I've seen and heard of, not gone away with, though—for ever pawing round you and very smarmy—there'd have been nothing doing. But what he really wants—most times anyhow—is just somebody to be with, to talk big to at dinner or late at night. He likes to sit on the edge of a bed, boasting a bit to round off the day. He's lonely really, for all his talk. He ought to have married again; his wife died when he was young and he hasn't forgotten her either. You can guess that pretty soon. I've weighed him up.'

'I can see the balance in your hand,' said Penderel. 'It's terrifying, but go on.'

'Now you're making fun of me,' she cried. 'I shan't tell you any more.'

It was queer, Penderel thought, how simple she became as soon as she talked directly to him, almost childish, whereas every time she spoke about anything else she surprised him. 'You must go on. I want to be terrified, and I only wish Porterhouse could hear this. It would open his eyes, though he's by no means a complacent fool about himself, judging from that little anecdote he told at the supper table. Tell me some more about him. Blow the masculine gaff.'

'Another thing about him is this. I fancy it's true about a lot of men too. When he asks me to go out with him or to go away with him, it's not so much that he really wants me there.' She stopped for a moment to think it out. 'What he really wants is not to be wanting somebody, d'you see? And that's not the same thing, is it?'

'Not by a thundering long chalk,' he told her. 'There's all the difference in the world between 'em.'

'Well, that's how it is, mostly, with him. He wants everything, you see, or thinks he does; and if he was by himself, knocking about town or staying at some swell seaside hotel, and he saw a lot of smart and pretty girls drifting round, he'd be as mad as blazes because he hadn't one. He wouldn't be able to eat his dinner for thinking about it. But if he has one too, there with him, staring him in the face if he cares to look across, it's all right then. And he's got somebody to show off and somebody to explain himself to and boast to, later on. That's where I come in, then. You see he happens to think I'm rather smart and fairly pretty. Probably you don't.'

'My dear Gladys, I think you're astonishingly pretty, a staggerer.' He didn't though; and it suddenly occurred to him that he had met quite a number of prettier girls—belonging to his own class, as people still said—who hadn't interested him at all, whereas this girl was most curiously attractive and exciting. Like a jolly good music-hall, he told himself. Well, whatever it was that drew him, it wasn't the mere look of her, though that was agreeable enough.

'You'd have to say that, wouldn't you? Well, I don't think I am very pretty, so there,' she said, quite earnestly. 'There's honesty for you.'

'Why, what's the trouble?'

'Oh, my face is too broad, to begin with, and my nose isn't right. My figure isn't either, not for these days when you ought to be very long and slender or a kind of boy.'

'They're all wrong. Don't you worry about them,' he remarked easily. 'I detest these death's head and crossbones women you see everywhere now.' He remembered, with pleasure, her fine sturdiness, now so much neighbouring warmth. But he was still wondering what it was that attracted him. All her obvious characteristics, of course, her courage and common sense and jolly impudence, floated on a deep rich stream, a Thames itself, of feminine vitality. She made Margaret Waverton seem nothing but a faintly freshened and animated mummy. And the Thames must have come into his mind, because, in some queer fashion, she was mixed up with his feeling about London. It was as if his thought of her danced all the time before a backcloth of the London scene, the roaringly human streets of Cockneydom—of buses and evening papers and oyster-bars and teashops and barrel organs and music-halls. That in itself, on such a night, might explain it all. But he had a feeling that it didn't.

She was asking him if he was listening. 'I've been hearing it some time,' she added.

'Hearing what?' He leaned forward a little, then looked at the vague rounded pallor of the face beside him, a mystery and an enchantment in its little darkness of eyes and lips.

'Outside. A kind of rushing noise.'

'I'd almost forgotten there was an outside. I can hear it now though. It's getting louder.'

'I should think it is. Sounds as if a river were coming down on us.' She gave a little shiver. 'What are you going to do?'

He was opening the door of the car. 'I'm going to see what's happening.'

'It sounds as if you want something to happen. I believe you do. If you're not careful, you'll make it happen.' There was a trace of real resentment in her tones.

He was out now on the floor of the shed, which sloped down towards the entrance. It seemed to be very wet. There was the noise of a great wash of water coming down, and already it seemed to be rushing past outside and creeping up the shed. It was difficult to see though, because the little lights of the car, which had been backed in at an angle, did not shine his way.

'I say, Roger.' Gladys was calling to him. It was queer to hear his Christian name like that, coming out of a dark place in a still unfamiliar voice. He felt as if he had suddenly dropped fifteen years and started over again. 'If you're going far, wait a minute,' she went on, 'because I'm coming with you.'

'I'm not going far,' he replied. 'Hardly a step farther.' The water was certainly coming into the shed; a flood had been loosed upon them from somewhere; there was the sound of a river roaring past. 'Look out,' he shouted. 'I'm coming back.' A sudden rush of water had swept round the corner like a little tidal wave. In a second it was nearly up to his knees, and the next moment he was climbing into the car again.

'Look at that,' he panted. 'Water's pouring into the place.' She leaned across and looked through the open door, while he tried to squeeze the water out of the bottom of his trousers.

'Why,' she cried, 'if it gets any higher it'll be in here soon.'

'In that case,' he grunted, still bending and trying to wring his trousers, 'you'll have to keep your feet on the cushions.'

She put out a hand. 'But suppose it gets higher and higher. My God, we're simply trapped here!'

He straightened himself now, brought his face close to hers and smiled at her through the deep dusk. 'We could get out somehow. Besides it can't rise much. It's bound to run away very quickly. It's rather amusing, don't you think?'

'Amusing!' He thought he saw her pull a face at him. 'I like your idea of amusement.'

His fingers touched something smooth and cold. It was the flask. He'd forgotten that too. 'There's just a spot left,' he said, shaking it. 'You have it.'

'Don't want it, thanks. Finish it yourself.'

'Shall I? Or shall I keep it for an emergency? Or is this an emergency? Tell me that.'

'You just said it wasn't, didn't you, Mr. Clever Man? But hurry up and finish it.' She leaned sideways against the cushions, her face turned towards him. 'I believe I want to go to sleep,' she yawned. 'I'll be off in a minute.' But inside she didn't feel a bit sleepy, all excited.

'If you went to sleep, something tremendous would happen and then you'd miss it.' He went rambling on while he slowly unscrewed the flask. 'You might wake up to find the water an inch from your chin and trout darting under your arms. Then again, of course, you might wake up to find that you weren't here at all but crossing Piccadilly Circus to catch the last Tube train.'

'And where would you be?'

'Nowhere at all. You'd have just dreamt me. You know how people you've seen only once or twice, as you saw me, pop up in your dreams and become quite important. Well, I should be one of them.'

'I don't want to wake up in Piccadilly Circus then.'

'Why?' He looked at her above the flask.

'Because I like you.'

'And by rain, by darkness, and by Sir Roderick Femm himself,' he cried, 'I like you too! I feel this is a great and solemn moment. You're sure you don't want any of this whisky?'

'Yes, I told you I didn't.'

'Then it must be put to an even nobler purpose than that of helping to rot my liver.'

'What are you going to do? Something crazy, I'll bet. I can see it coming.'

'I'm going to sacrifice it—the last drop too, mind, and I'm coldish—to celebrate this moment. I'll address a few remarks, we won't call it a prayer, to the gods, and then I'll pour it out as an offering, a libation. How's this?' He sat bolt upright. 'Oh, gods of light and beauty and happiness,' he began, in rich, vibrating tones, 'crowned with flowers in eternal May, hear the cry that comes from the little world that you have left so long unvisited. Behold two mortals whose hearts were fashioned for your service but who sit in a darkness within a darkness, homeless, lost, the black water rising round them——'

'I shall want to weep in a minute,' she interrupted. 'You ought to go on the stage, Roger.'

'I am on the stage, Gladys. I'm on it all the time, but only wander about trying to remember what my next cue is, and what the play's about, and wondering who the devil can be in the audience. But you've ruined my exhortation now. I'll have to trust to the libation. Here goes.' He held out the flask and raised his voice again. 'Accept this offering, all that we can give, the last drops of our golden spirit.' The flask was solemnly emptied into the water just outside the door.

'Well, d'you feel any better now?' she enquired as he returned to her side. She was smiling at him.

He had twisted round, so that they were sitting face to face, and now his hands shot out to clasp her arms. 'Do you know, I believe I do,' he cried. 'I think they'd had a glance at us—those gods, I mean—even before I made the libation, and now they may really take notice of us. When I come to think of it, I've felt depressed only once to-night, and that's almost a record.'

'When was that?' She pressed gently against the hands that were still curved loosely round her arms.

'Oh, before you arrived; just after we went into the house. I can remember the very moment. I'd been left alone, and suddenly everything went as hollow as hell—perhaps you don't know the feeling?'

'Don't I though! I've had weeks of it, when it's a bother to breathe, let alone get up and wash and do your hair and dress and eat——'

'And walk about and talk to people or even look at their silly eyes, and then undress and crawl into bed, to try and sleep, and after that begin it all over again. I know. Still, I shouldn't have thought you would.'

'Well, I do,' she said gravely. 'Why did you think I didn't?'

'You seemed to have so much life in you, good red stuff,' he replied, considering her. 'I couldn't imagine anything downing you for more than a minute. I don't believe it does.'

'Oh yes, it does.' She nodded her head, round-eyed, like a child. Then she laughed. 'For that matter,' she cried, 'I shouldn't have thought it of you either. I never met anybody so full of beans. Why, even when you're saying how miserable you are, you seem to be enjoying yourself a lot more than most people are when they think they're really happy for once. Look at Sir Bill there. He wouldn't admit he wasn't ever enjoying himself, but at the top of his form, with a pint or two of champagne tucked away inside him, he's a damn sight more miserable than you are when you talk as if you were nearly dead. So there, Mister Roger.'

'Ah, but'—and he shook his head—'to-night's different. That's what I'm really trying to tell you.'

'I'd risk every night being different, with you. Not that you aren't fed up, of course. It didn't take me long to see that. And then that story of yours. That got over all right with me, I can tell you. But you've no need to sit about, thinking it out over and over again or doping yourself. You're not really that sort. I know. You're full of fight and fun. I'm a bit like that myself but not so much as you are, and that's why I like you or partly why. Only I'm not clever like you and that makes it easier for me.'

'I'm just not quite so clever as a ten-year-old retriever,' he protested. 'And that's not modesty either. I don't even want to be clever. I've met some of the clever ones, and they make me sick.'

She stirred and then moved a little closer to him. 'Why don't you do something?'

'What's this?' he exclaimed softly. 'Good advice?'

'Sounds like it, doesn't it? I expect you're thinking it's damned cheek, coming from me.'

'No, I'm not. It couldn't come from a better person; I wouldn't have it from anybody else, I believe. But what do you mean exactly?'

Before she replied, she slid a hand up the cushion and then rested her cheek against it. He found something curiously moving in that little action, seen vaguely in the gloom of their little covered place. It was one of those things that women carry over from childhood. And now she was beginning to explain herself in that funny little voice of hers, which had been hastily shedding acquired accents and becoming more piquant all the time they had been talking together.

'What I mean is this,' she began. 'Have a pop at something. Start something fresh. Take a chance again. But try something you haven't tried before. You can call it good advice if you like, and it is for your own good I'm telling you; but I don't mean you ought to go to night-school or keep hens or put five shillings a week in the Post Office Savings Bank. You can work the confidence trick or run a roulette board, if it comes to a pinch—though I can't see you doing anything like that—but the thing is, do something. If you think everything's all wrong—about the war and all that—you could at least take a soapbox round and spout at street corners, like the Bolshies or socialists or whatever they are. Anyhow, do something, and then you won't know yourself.'

He'd had a glimpse of the essentially feminine point of view. We're tremendously important as persons, he said to himself, but they're just detached and amused about all our antics, whether we're running a roulette or weighing the sun. We're still spending half our time, in their eyes, scrambling in and out of the big nursery cupboard. Gladys plainly thought his grand deep philosophic pessimism—which she was obviously ready to lump with socialism and relativity and psychoanalysis and fascism and anything else she may have heard about—could be disposed of by talking it out, being only so much steam to be let off. And perhaps it was so much steam to be let off. Perhaps she was wiser than he was. It was all very fascinating; and one thing having this point of view described in books and quite another thing coming across it like this, suddenly seeing a fantastically coloured searchlight flashing out of a familiar sky. Here at his elbow was really another world; and it was soft, warm, and breathing, a person, somebody you could talk and laugh and cry with, not so very different in most things, indeed strangely like you. His thought, having raced round this little circle, suddenly stopped.

'And if you're cross now,' she was saying, 'then you're no sport, and I don't like you.'

'I was never less cross,' he cried. 'The fact is, I'm all excited. Either there's something very heady about a car that's standing still or throwing that whisky away has made me drunk.' He really did feel oddly exultant all of a sudden. 'I think the spell must be working. Life's suddenly changed from being a damned long dusty road into an enormous hamper, and I feel as if I'm trying to lift the lid now. Gladys, I want to give you a colossal hug.'

Her hands came down in front of her and then fluttered towards him. 'Well,' she said calmly, 'if that's how you feel, go on.'

She was in his arms and her face was tilted back, a few inches away. They kissed. Then her hand was passed over his cheek, and his arms tightened about her and they kissed again. It was all done very quietly and comfortably, without any of the blind fumbling and straining of a new passion, yet it had not only meaning but intensity. This intensity, however, like a slant of sunlight, had passed through a mellowing atmosphere of large friendliness.

Now, her hands pressing against him, she gently pushed herself away. Penderel drew a long breath. He wasn't bewildered, he wasn't ecstatic; he was suddenly and solidly happy. He felt enormously rich.

'I didn't mean that, you know,' she remarked, 'when I said you ought to do something.'

'That's a pity. No, it isn't.' It was funny. He was cool enough, and yet his voice wasn't. It was hoarse, unsteady. 'Well, I will do something now. I'll start this week.'

'Listen, Roger.' She put a hand on his arm. 'Why don't you come to London?'

'I will. As a matter of fact, I'm on my way there now. That sounds damned odd, when you think of it.'

'You must think I'm rushing it.' She was very serious now. 'But I can't help it. I feel I must, while we're here and it's quiet and—Oh!—I don't know. But listen. Do you—will you—want to see me again?'

His hands went out, but she caught and held them. 'No, never mind about that, now. Tell me, honestly and truly, do you?'

'Of course I do!' he cried. 'What a question! Why, you're the very person I'm going up to see, though I didn't know it when I began this journey. But then I didn't know anything. When do we get there? Anyhow, we'll begin with dinner the very first night, that is, if Sir William doesn't object. What about him?'

'Don't be silly. He doesn't matter. He can fade out. He's done that already.'

'So he has,' he assented. 'And it's a comforting thought. But what's this about town?'

'I want to see you too. And I want to help if you'll start again. I'll do anything, everything.'

His mind went blundering after her. 'Do you mean——' he began.

'Don't you see what I mean?' she broke in, with a whispered vehemence. 'I'll do everything. Oh, it sounds crazy, I know. Don't think I'm always like this. I've never been like this before. But the girl from the chorus you've met in the middle of the night is telling you she'll live with you if you want her to, and there you have it. She's gone mad and is flinging herself at you.'

'And he's trying to fling himself at her,' he cried, clasping her arms. An idea was fermenting in his mind. Why shouldn't they try it together? They'd nothing to lose, at least he hadn't, and everything to gain. It was delightfully crazy, this idea of his, which wasn't identical with hers, much crazier. But he hadn't tested the strength of hers yet. 'You're absolutely regal, Gladys; you take my breath away. But listen to me a minute——'

'Are you going to tell me you don't want me?' she demanded. 'Because you've only to nod and it'll save you the trouble.'

'No, I'm not,' he replied hastily. 'Something quite different.'

'Then I know what it is,' she went on, 'and I'm going to tell you. You were just going to point out that you hadn't much money and didn't exactly know where you were going to earn any and that I'd have a damned thin time, weren't you? I knew you were. Well, that doesn't matter. If you really like me enough, we can have some fun together and manage somehow. To begin with, I can get a job. I really have been in the chorus, you know—though lately I've been resting—though I've not had much from Bill, you needn't think it; he's not been keeping me really—and I can go back to the chorus. If there's nothing doing there, I can easily get a job of some sort—there's a girl I know managing a milliner's who'd get me into the shop. And we'd find a cheap little flat, high up, somewhere not too far out, and if you found anything at all to do, we'd manage all right. I know I'd be pretty rotten, and you probably wouldn't be comfortable at first. I can't do much—something quick and easy on a gas-ring is about my limit in cooking—but I'd try and I'd be happy so long as you didn't curse me too often. I know what it means, of course; I'm not a kid. Living like that with anybody else but you would be little hell; but with you it would be all different—there'd be fun and excitement all the time—and we'd go roaming round together and talk and talk about everything, just as we've been doing to-night, and we wouldn't feel lost and lonely any more. I know I'm not the sort of girl you used to think about—like that other one—but I understand; and if you ever got depressed I'd tease you out of it and then love you hard—Oh! you must think I'm silly.' A little choked cry, and she had flung her arms round him and was pressing her face against his.

'My dear, my dear,' he found himself saying. He saw the two of them crazily garreting it together somewhere above the bus tops; laughing or grousing together if nothing came off; jubilant over the occasional windfalls; rushing one another into life. He was holding her close now, was protective, soothing; yet all the time he had a dim feeling that it was he who was finding comfort, sustenance itself, in this happy weight in his arms. Here was the way back into things. But he wouldn't sneak up to share her attic. His own idea, mad as it seemed, was better than that. They'd get married, risk all and then plunge in together. No doubt people were right, he'd wanted the moon; now he'd start again and simply want cheese; and perhaps in the end he'd find that the moon was made of cheese after all.

He put a hand on her hair and gently tilted back her face so that he could kiss her again. 'It's a great idea, Gladys,' he told her, 'and you're wonderful, and we'll make it all happen. Only my idea improves on yours, though you'll probably think it crazy.'

'Tell me,' she whispered. 'What is it?'

'Let's go back first, and then I will.' She must hear it back in the house, with other people not far away, where she could test it. Anything was plausible here, in this tiny odd world they seemed to have created for themselves. 'We've been too long away as it is. We'll go back now.'

'No, no. You want to leave me.' He felt her body stiffen in his arms.

'I don't. Not ever. But we must see what the others are doing. They're probably asleep.' He couldn't help feeling that they weren't, though. 'Then we'll talk it all out. I've a special reason for wanting to finish it off there.'

'All right.' She drew back but kept her eyes fixed on his. Then, after a pause, she went on: 'But are you sure——?' The question died away. Her voice was dubious; her stare was dubious, sombre. He was instantly visited by a curious mixed feeling of alarm and shame. It had occurred to her that she really knew nothing about him. And he knew nothing about her. They were strangers, staring through the dusk at one another. Voices, questioning eyes, the electric contact of flesh, and you seemed to know everything—a turn of the wheel, a click, and you knew nothing. The old despair returned; he was trapped again. Without thinking what he was doing, he took hold of her hand and the next moment it had given him a warm hard squeeze. At the same time a thought arrived, just as if it had been squeezed into him.

'Why,' he cried aloud, 'it's all bosh!'

'What!' She withdrew her hand instantly. 'What d'you mean?'

'Sorry! I didn't mean about us, you know, though we come into it. I'd been thinking and had just made a discovery.'

She regarded him indulgently. 'You'd better get it off your chest, hadn't you? Go on. I'm listening.'

'We all get on a romantic switchback—up and down, up and down all the time.' He was talking to himself rather than to her. 'First we can know everything and it's wonderful, then we can know nothing and it's all rotten. Just as if there wasn't a way in between! There always is, all the time, and we're simply too damned proud and lazy and egoistical to find it and go down it. The thing we won't bother with is just plain common sense. It frightens us. It makes us seem less important. Why, after all, Gladys, I know you——'

'Do you though?' she interrupted. 'That's what I've just been wondering about. You don't really, do you? I don't really know you, though I seem to better than anybody. That's funny, isn't it?' She was very eager, excited.

'Yes, I do,' he replied sturdily. 'I don't know all about you, but I feel I know a devil of a lot. If I've made it up, I've made it up, and that's that. But I can go on learning. There's a truth to come out.' He was excited himself now and sat up as if to proclaim his discovery to the world. He felt as if he had turned a corner. 'That's what we really don't want to believe, that there's a truth to come out. We don't want to sit tight, wait, and learn anything. We pretend we're above sensible compromise, when all the time we're below it. All this disillusion's egoistical bunkum.'

'I dare say it is, though I don't know what you mean. I never knew anybody who went on at such a rate. And who are you talking about, with your "we pretend" this and "we do" that?'

She wasn't eager now, but amused and worshipping, as if he had just done something rather clever with a box of bricks. 'Now, who d'you mean?'

'Oh—er—people like me, I suppose, gloomy young asses,' he told her. 'I speak,' he added, with mock pompousness, 'for my own generation, though whether you are a member of that generation or not, my dear Gladys, I am not prepared to say.'

'You're prepared to say anything, if you ask me.' She leaned forward. 'And you're a funny boy and I don't know why I'm bothering myself about you.' Her cheek was lightly brushed across his and a hand passed over his head.

'That was benediction,' he said. 'Now we must go. We'll begin again—never to end—in the house. Ready?' He rose from the seat and discovered that his feet were very cold and his legs were cramped.

'No, Roger, no!' She was holding his arm. 'Don't let's go back there. Let's stay here.'

He turned to stare at her. 'Why, what's the matter? We can finish the night comfortably there. It may be queerish, but at least there's a fire. Why don't you want to go?'

'Because there's something—oh! I dunno. I'm silly I suppose. P'raps it's just because I don't want to leave this funny little place—I'd almost forgotten it's the back seat of a car; if you've been happy in a place, no matter what it's like, you don't want to leave it, do you? It's a risk moving on, isn't it? I expect that's it.' But she sounded very doubtful.

He switched off the small lights of the car, found the torch, and stepped out into about a foot of water. 'We shall have to wade back,' he told her, flashing the light inside. 'I wonder if I could carry you.'

'No, you couldn't,' she replied. 'I'm an awful weight.' Nevertheless he swooped upon her, just as she was getting out, and went splashing forward with her in his arms, contriving at the same time to send the light of the torch before them. That tiny fantastic journey was for them both like the mingling of a

nightmare, in which all familiar things suddenly lost their iden-
tity, crawling into nothingness or taking on shapes of terror,
and one of those clear dreams in which the enchanted heart
recognises and claims its most secret desires as if they were
children long-lost. Here the dream, their sense of one another,
their nearness and warmth, threaded through the nightmare
made up of the sight of that obliterating black water, the air
that seemed like hanging crape, the corners of the house
that gleamed sharply in the light of his torch like naked bone,
and a fear, swelling beyond sensible dimensions, lest his foot
should slip and they should fall. More than once she protested,
but he would not put her down, and twice he had to rest,
leaning heavily against the wall of the house, with one arm
still holding her tight. Wet and aching, he was staggering now
past a lighted window. The door could not be far away. Gladys
threw out a hand, found the wall, and steadied them both,
wondering all the while at his odd determination to indulge
his whim at any cost. She found herself slipping down out of
his arms, and her feet touched the highest of the three steps.
He came scrambling up after her, sank back against the side of
the door, and fought for his breath. And now, for the second
time that night, he had his hand upon the knocker.

CHAPTER XI

Once inside the room, Margaret peeped round Philip's shoulder. It was a large room and Margaret had a vague impression that it was full of lovely old things; but their candle, the only light there, merely illuminated a tiny space and then simply conjured the rest of the room, the circling darkness, into rich dusk, in which there wavered and shone, from unseen polished surfaces, little reflections of its flame. Thus she saw a background of shadows and some twinkling points of light, like a night sky. Then she stepped out from behind Philip and cleared her eyes. They were in a very large bedroom, heavy with old furniture. The bed itself was a huge shadowy affair, a great four-poster, canopied with dark curtains at the head.

A voice came from the gloom there, and they moved forward. The light now fell on a hand resting on the counterpane, the hand of a very old man, a featherweight of brittle bone. 'Who are you?' the voice was asking. Leaving Philip behind, still holding the candle, Margaret drew nearer to the bed. Now she could dimly see the man who was lying there, could see his white hair and long white beard; his face was vague yet curiously luminous; it moved a little; he must be looking at her. 'Who are you?' The question was repeated. Even here, his voice seemed nothing more than a whisper.

Philip had heard it too, but remained where he was for the moment, feeling sure that Margaret wanted to reply herself, to explain why they were there. He was more than content that she should. Who were they? It was a question that came very aptly, pointedly, ironically from that bed.

'I am Mrs. Waverton and this is my husband,' Margaret was saying. 'Are you Sir Roderick Femm?'

'Yes . . . Sir Roderick . . .' The voice came as faintly as before;

the words might have been spoken by the very air of that dim place.

Margaret nodded and tried to smile at that blur of face with its ghostly sheen. 'We have had to take shelter here for the night. There has been a very bad storm. We came in because we thought we heard you calling. Can we get you anything?'

The hand that had been lying on the counterpane seemed to raise itself, and, like something clumsily floating, it moved uncertainly towards the right of the bed, where there was a little table. It's horrible, Philip thought as he stared; it's like watching a ghost, no, worse than that, a spirit coming back to try and make the old, rusty, creaky machinery of the body work again. The real Sir Roderick had already retired from life. Yet he hadn't; he was wanting something; yes, he was still wanting something; and that made it all the worse. What was he saying?

'Water,' came the whisper. 'Glass empty . . . Water over there . . .'

Margaret had heard and understood. 'Yes, I'll get you some,' she said, and taking up the glass from the little table, she went in the direction the hand had pointed and filled the glass from a carafe that she found on the top of a chest of drawers there. She still trembled slightly and felt a little heart-sick, but the action gave her a certain feeling of warmth and confidence. Returning with the glass, she put it into the awaiting hand, a frail curve of bone. 'Can you take it yourself,' she enquired gently, 'or shall I give it to you?'

'I can—do it—myself,—thank you.' The hand closed round the glass and slowly raised it. For one second the water caught and held the candle-light and became liquid gold. The old man's head came forward shakily, and they had a glimpse of a great curved nose, shaggy white brows, and wasted cheeks. Somehow it didn't seem difficult to believe that he had once been easily the tallest and strongest and handsomest of the family, a magnificent figure. He had been a great man once, they had said. No doubt it was true; and now he could hardly raise the glass to his lips, and when he did at last succeed in drinking some of the water, spilling it into his mouth, it seemed a triumphant achievement.

The water appeared to revive him, however, for he was able to replace the glass on the table, and though his head sank back again upon the piled pillows, into the deep shadow of the curtains, there seemed to be a faint trace of animation in his movements. But his voice remained the same, a ghostly whisper, a mere breath in the air. Yet it was he who spoke first, before Margaret could ask him if there was anything else he wanted.

'What was—the noise there?' he asked.

Margaret explained, very briefly and as lightly as she could, what had happened outside. She had stepped back now and was standing by the side of Philip.

'Morgan—is a savage,' they heard. 'It was—the drink though. We have had to keep him here'—and the voice trailed away into a long pause—'because of my brother. I must—apologise for him.'

This was the master of the house, though he seemed to whisper to them across an open grave, and here were accents they had not caught before under this roof. It was queer how this little speech appeared to lift a weight, the pressure of something unnamed, from their minds.

'Did you say—you were husband and wife?' The whisper came again, after a brief silence, filled with departing images.

'Yes, we are,' Margaret replied, very simply, like a child; and Philip felt her hand on his arm. She couldn't help it; answering that had somehow been like another marriage ceremony, graver than that other in the little church at Otterwell. She thought of that, and then innumerable little pictures flashed across her mind: the two of them dining together that night at the Gare de Lyon; then going through the dust and faerie of Provence; the tiny flat in Doughty Street, with Philip painting the fireplace; the Hampstead house and Betty in the garden;

and with all that had not been shared since flitting darkly through her mind like a bad dream.

He spoke again out of the shadow. 'You are fortunate—very fortunate. I never married. There was—so much to do—but I came—to be very lonely—at last.' In spite of the frequent pauses, there was no gasping nor obvious effort in his speech, and its faint drip-drip of words gave it a strangely remote, oracular quality. He wasn't conversing, Philip felt; he was too old for that; there was only time to call faintly from the darkening hillside. Philip didn't want to move nor even to speak; he only wanted to stand there, staring across the flame of the candle, listening and wondering.

There was a slight stirring in the bed and the hand groped its way towards the little table. Margaret started forward out of her dream and gave him the glass again. This time he leaned further forward than before, and after he had sipped and the glass had been replaced he remained where he was, looking at them, with the light falling on his face. Years and disease had played havoc there, and his eyes were hidden by his thick brows; but, over and above all that, there was a marked difference between him and the other two Femms. They had only a moment, however, in which to return his scrutiny, that curiously impersonal stare of old age, for no sooner had he spoken again than he sank back into the shadow. 'You shouldn't have come here,' he whispered, and then vanished from the light.

'Oh, I'm sorry,' said Margaret, hastily apologetic. 'But we couldn't help it, you know. We were absolutely cut off and had no other place to shelter in.' She flashed a glance at Philip.

'It wasn't a mere matter of comfort,' he put in, 'but of escaping from real danger. There was a landslide and a flood.' He felt as if he were earnestly addressing nothing, as if Sir Roderick had departed and would not return until he was ready to make another remark.

He made another now. But first they saw the hand on the counterpane lifted, presumably to cut short their explanations and apologies. 'I'm afraid—you misunderstand me,' he said very slowly. 'You make me—seem inhospitable. I was never that—never.' Here they caught the dry husk of a laugh, a ghostly and incredible sound. 'This house—was always filled with guests—at one time—years ago—many years.' They could almost hear those years rustling by in the long pauses. And Margaret suddenly thought of Rachel Femm and the young men who came riding in and the women smothered in silks and scents who had laughed at Miss Femm. This room, the whole house, was dimmed and thick with presences, haunted.

'I wish—I could have—received you,' the whisper, so curiously remote, began again. 'But you see, I am—old—ailing—tired now. I have done—with life. No—not quite done. There is always something—we want. Now—it is—a drink of water.'

'Do you want one now?' Margaret asked, reaching out for the glass. She did not choose to see beyond the simple need.

'Thank you,' he said, without emphasis; and the hand went fumbling out. In that gesture, even more than in the two whispered words, Philip seemed to discover a deliberate and frugal irony, an irony that would have been simply terrifying at any other time. Now, after so many of his thoughts had gone down this dusty way, it came strangely to reassure him. He was able to cling to the fact that something looked out above the wreckage, unconquered, serene.

Once more refreshed by a sip or two of water their host returned to the shadows and spoke again. 'No doubt—when you came—they told you. I don't know what—they told you.'

'We were told,' said Margaret, very quietly, 'that you were an invalid and in bed.'

'That is—only the beginning. Was that all?'

Remembering so many things, Margaret felt confused, and looked at Philip. But Philip, not knowing how to begin to answer the question, shook his head. He felt as if the old man were listening carefully to their silence and would soon reply to it.

This he did. 'You have seen—my brother, Horace—and

my sister? And Morgan—you have seen him. You have been thinking—this is a strange house—a strange family. You may have wondered—whether you did well—in coming—even for shelter—out of the storm—into this house—this old dark house. I should like—to tell you everything—to explain. But there's no time—no time to explain. I like to see you—standing there—very young, younger than you think—and I haven't seen—anybody like you—so young—for many a year. I had almost forgotten. . . .' His voice floated into a silence. They waited, unstirring, for him to come groping out of his reverie. Then he went on, more brokenly now: 'I could have told you—a long story—but no time. And talking—tires me.'

'I'm sure it does,' said Margaret. 'Please don't trouble. We're only disturbing you.'

He raised his hand a few inches, as if gently commanding her to be silent. 'Terrible misfortune,' he whispered, 'came—to this house. First death—very early—for two—a young boy—then a girl, Rachel. Then—after years—something broke down—the life ran out—there came—a strain of madness.' He broke off and there was silence again.

Standing here in this shadowy room, listening to this curiously remote voice, Philip thought, might seem more fantastic than creeping on that landing above or fighting with Morgan outside, than hearing Miss Femm's screaming or watching Mr. Femm's hollow eyes; yet he could not help feeling as if a light were about to shine through the house, as if he were coming out at the end of a long tunnel.

'It didn't touch me—this madness,' he began again. 'At least—I don't think—it did—though there was a time—years and years ago—before you were born—when I was wild—did mad things—I don't know. It touched—all the others—various ways—different degrees—but shut them all off somehow—stopped them all really living—passed them through a little death—half-way—then set them going again—with something dead inside. You have seen my brother Horace—still sharp—a kind of cunning—but all empty and brittle—a shell—with something gone—for ever. And then—Rebecca—poor creature—she may have troubled you—nearly deaf—shut off—everything missed—and now with a God—a God behind her—a God who is deaf—vengeful—half-crazed—like she is. Don't let her trouble you—yet have pity on her—you are young—don't anger her—only for one night. But you have seen—the last of her perhaps—is she asleep? Is it—very late? I feel—we all ought to be asleep.'

'Yes, it's very late,' Margaret told him. 'Wouldn't you like to go to sleep now?' But this was only a little part of herself, a little mechanical part, that was talking, though pity for him remained. The rest of her was darkly bewildered and on edge. The soft slow pat-patter of his voice and this shuttered room and thick, haunted air were beating down her spirit.

'Not yet,' came the voice again, answering her question. 'There'll be—plenty of time to sleep—soon. There's still something left—to tell you—for there may be—danger.'

'Danger!' she cried, shooting a glance at Philip. Was he thinking of Morgan? Was he thinking at all? Perhaps it was he who was mad, far crazier than the others, and was dragging them and the whole house into some long nightmare spun out of loneliness and pain.

Philip found his voice now. Here, he felt, he could ask questions and be answered. 'Danger? Do you mean from Morgan?'

'No—not directly. We keep him here—because of my brother, Saul.'

'Saul?' But something was swiftly taking shape in Philip's mind even as he cried out the name. That door.

'Ah!—they have said nothing—about Saul?' It came with maddening deliberation.

'No, no; what about him?' Margaret tore the question out of a tormented mind. Why didn't he hurry, hurry?

'It was on him—there fell—the heaviest blow. A raging madness. At times—he is a dangerous maniac. Always he wanted—to destroy—to wipe out everything—so that life—could be made—over again. There was—you see—a kind of nobility—in Saul—but now his mind—lives—in darkness. Not always—but the madness returns—to destroy him—the destroyer.'

'Where is he?' asked Margaret, shakily. The question was directed at the bed but actually she was looking at Philip, who was now nodding his head and frowning as he always did when he thought he knew something important.

'I know where he is,' Philip announced. 'I've heard him and seen his room, at least the door of it. He's upstairs, isn't he, behind those bolts?'

'Yes—he is there,' Sir Roderick replied. 'He's been locked in now—for several days—has been very violent—I understand. Only Morgan—can look after him—such times. He doesn't attempt—to hurt Morgan—even during—the worst attacks. And Morgan—half savage—very superstitious—is devoted to him. Otherwise—Saul couldn't have—stayed here.' Obviously he could only speak with an effort now, and the pauses seemed to be longer between each whispered phrase. It seemed to be sheer weakness, however, and not actual pain that was mastering him.

'But if he did get out, we could lock ourselves in somewhere, couldn't we?' Margaret herself was whispering now. She was cold and felt all hollow inside.

'You could,' came the answer, so softly. 'But if he—found his way—downstairs—to a fire—or lights—or even matches—I think—he might set fire—to the house. He has tried—before—a sacrifice—cleansing by fire—he called it. Up there—in his room—there is nothing—no fire nor matches—that is why—we had electric lighting.'

Margaret bit her lips. She wanted to grab hold of Philip and run away, anywhere, back into the darkness and rain, through the flood if necessary.

Philip concentrated his mind, the prey of huge trampling images, with desperate swiftness. Something had to come yet. This voice, calling so weakly from some remote high place, seemed to be letting down a fine silken cord; it floated before him, a silver thread in the mirk; and he felt he had to grasp it, hold on to it, or the world was lost. 'But those bolts will hold, surely,' he cried. 'That door seemed strong enough.'

'It is—but this is—what I wanted—to tell you. If Morgan— is so bad—if he's not asleep—or come—to his senses—I think he might—open the door. You will have—to watch him.'

'Philip!' Margaret gave a little scream, and he felt her hands fumbling on his coat. Why hadn't he thought of that before? He must see if Morgan was still there—though there hadn't been much time for him to recover—and then find the others and decide what to do. 'Stay here,' he said to Margaret. 'I'll go and have a look at him.' He dashed out into the landing, and she followed as far as the door.

A few steps in the flickering candle-light and he saw that Morgan was not there. 'Morgan!' he cried, without thinking. Before he could reach the place where Morgan had been lying, where the broken lamp and its splintered glass told their tale, a door on the left opened and there peered out a face like paper. It was Mr. Femm.

'He's just gone,' Mr. Femm gabbled reedily. 'Gone upstairs. I heard him go. He's gone to let Saul out, I know he has. And Saul's mad, mad. Get out of the way. Wait for him downstairs. There are three of you. Wait for him there. Kill him!' And the face was gone, the door banged to and locked.

Philip hastened back down the landing and found Margaret swaying in the doorway. 'You heard that?' he cried, pushing her forward into the room. 'He may be letting him out.'

'What are we to do?' she gasped. 'Can't we stay here? Lock the door?'

'No, we can't do that. Mustn't let him loose downstairs. And the others don't know.' He saw there was a key inside the door. 'We shall have to get downstairs at once. I can't go and tackle the two of them up there.'

The whisper came from the bed again. 'Yes, go. Lock me in—and take the key—with you.'

Philip drew back the door, took out the key, gave the candle to Margaret and motioned her forward. She turned swiftly in the doorway, however, and called back: 'Oh, are you sure you'll be all right?'

'Yes—all right—take care—good luck.' The voice seemed to come from miles away, through a great darkness, the last friendly whisper of humanity. The next moment they were outside, with the door locked behind them.

There was a moment's silence, during which their ears seemed to catch the last faint vibrations of that voice from the darkened bed. They were hurrying towards the stairs, but they had not gone more than a few paces when the silence was broken. A yell of laughter went pealing through the house. It came from somewhere above, perhaps through an open door. It was the sudden laughter of madness. At the sound of it, the mind, hearing its own knell ringing in an empty sky, ran affrighted, and the heart, awaking out of its dream of peace and kindness, stood still.

CHAPTER XII

Sir William heard the knocking again, sat up and rubbed his eyes, stared at the door for a minute, recovering his wits, then marched across and opened it wide. 'Hello!' he cried, as the bedraggled pair staggered past him into the room. 'And where the devil have you two been?' He followed them across to the fire.

'It's a long story,' Penderel began; his face was pale and a little drawn, but his eyes were dancing.

'Then cut it short,' Sir William growled. What a wild young devil he looks, he told himself; something between a gunman and a fiddler.

Penderel was busy taking off his boots. 'Well, you see, I went out to Waverton's car to get my flask——'

Here Gladys broke in: 'And I went with him to the door, and then I was shut out and couldn't get in, and so I found him in the car and we sat there and talked.' She looked at him rather defiantly, very bright-eyed. 'And we've had to wade through a lake to get back.'

Penderel was padding across the room in his stockinged feet, in search of his bag. 'Why, what's been happening here?' he asked.

'God knows. I don't. I've been hanging about here, waiting for somebody to come or something to happen. And just look at the place. It gets on your nerves. Every time I've wakened up I've had a shock.'

'But where are they all?' Gladys looked bewildered.

'Don't ask me. Can't tell you.' Sir William blew out his breath impatiently. 'I'll tell you what I do know. The lights went out. Waverton and what's-his-name—Femm—went off to find a lamp. They're finding it yet. Then that little screeching woman—she's as mad as a hatter, that woman, and

I hope I've seen the last of her—well, she wanted someone to shut a window. I did that and listened to her raving. Then she dug out a little lamp and I came back with it. That's the one.' He pointed to the tiny oil lamp burning on the table. 'Good job I brought it, too, or I'd have been in the dark. Well, when I came back, Mrs. Waverton had disappeared. I didn't want to start roaming round the house, so waited here by the fire. Must have dozed off. Thought I heard a crash somewhere, but may have dreamt it. Woke up though, but nobody came, so dozed off again, and next thing I heard was you knocking.'

Gladys exchanged glances with Penderel, who was coming back with some clothes over his arm. 'We must investigate this,' he said cheerfully. He moved over to a door opposite the staircase, to the left of the fireplace, a door that had not been opened yet. 'I wonder what happens in here. Could I go in, do you think?'

'Why?' Gladys was alarmed. 'What are you going to do?'

He grinned at her. 'Change my trousers.' He looked a little longer and his grin changed to a smile. 'Back in a minute.' The door closed behind him.

Sir William had turned quickly and was now holding Gladys lightly at arms length. 'What's the idea, Gladys? Amusing yourself, or love at first sight?'

She met his look bravely. 'It's real, Bill. You won't mind. You're too decent—and friendly. You ought to be glad.'

'Oh!—ought I?—you monkey! Sharp work, I must say. But—tell me—is it—both sides? What about him?'

She nodded gravely. Then suddenly her face lit up, and the sentimental boy who still lived on inside him felt as if he were catching a glimpse of sunrise in a lost world. It was indeed the most exquisite sensation she had ever given him, and he struggled hard not to enjoy it. 'I can't begin to tell you——' she began.

'Then don't,' he broke in, still at odds with himself.

Then he softened: 'No, go on. Let's hear all about it.'

She came nearer and put a hand on his arm. 'There isn't

time. But listen, Bill. It's no good pretending to be cross. I know you don't mean it. He's coming to town, to be with me. I want him to do something, put his back into it, and I know he will. You saw what he was like before, absolutely fed up, not caring a damn about anything. Well, I'm knocking that on the head, knocked it already.'

'Ah, the old game, eh?' He chuckled over her. 'Reforming him already, are we? Then it's serious.'

'It is, but it's going to be a hell of a lark too. Now you've got to help. You can easily find him a job, you've plenty to spare.'

'For solid downright cheek,' he exclaimed, 'give me a young woman who thinks herself in love.'

'Now don't be silly. It isn't cheek, and you know it's not. Besides, he's tremendously clever, you can see that, and full of push and go. Hurry up and say you will, he's coming back.'

'Well, I'll see,' he muttered, receiving her quick glance of gratitude. 'I'll have a talk to him.' He could see that door opening behind him in her very eyes.

'The world's great age begins anew.' Penderel's voice rang through that dim place. His sudden high spirits seemed to light it up. 'Gladys, Sir William, I've changed my socks and trousers—in the dark too, mind you—and now I'm a new man. I don't know what there was in that room. I just stood behind the door. Perhaps it was full of monsters, all watching me. By the way, you've been talking about me. I see it written in your faces. Your silence tells me all. I could even guess what you've been saying. Here's the evidence. Sir William knows, in his heart of hearts, that even if he would, I wouldn't.'

'You've been listening,' Gladys cried, making a face at him.

'I only heard three words,' he replied. 'The rest was intuition, for which we men are now becoming famous. We may not be able to argue, to debate, to reason, but we know. Well, my first step in this new life is to locate the missing Wavertons. If necessary we could all creep round the house until we heard Waverton's snore. Then we'll sing Sir William here to sleep again, and after that, you and I, Gladys, will find a corner and talk and talk, at least I'll talk and you'll probably sleep. The dawn, which must be somewhere on its way, will find me talking. Mr. Femm will come down to breakfast—but you can't imagine him at breakfast, can you?—in fact, you can't imagine breakfast here at all. Try to think of it.'

'I can't,' said Gladys, decisively. Then, after a short pause, very slowly and clearly she added, 'I hate this house.'

'Rum old place certainly.' This from Sir William. Penderel said nothing. He was staring curiously at Gladys, who was strolling away.

She stopped. 'It's the worst house I've ever been in. And that's saying a lot, as you'd admit if you knew anything about professional digs. There's something about it—I dunno—like a bad smell—something putrid.' She walked on and then stood looking at the staircase.

Sir William took Penderel to one side. 'No business of mine, of course,' he said gruffly, 'but what's this about you and Gladys?'

'I'll let you into the secret,' Penderel returned gaily. 'And, by the way, isn't it funny that officially, according to the book of words, you and I ought to be totally incapable of talking to one another like ordinary human beings? At the very least, we ought to be embarrassed to the stuttering point.'

'Well, I'll tell you something.' Sir William was emphatic. 'That's just what I am.'

'Not you!' cried Penderel. 'And I'm not even pretending to be. I'm going to marry Gladys, that is if she'll have me; I haven't asked her yet. And that's the idea.'

'Most people'd tell you that you were either a fool or a hero,' Sir William remarked, rather heavily. This rising tide of high spirits made him feel heavy. But he was trying to deal honestly with the youngster, who wasn't a bad sort in his own scatter-brained fashion. 'But I don't say so, though you may be both for all I know. It'll probably be the best day's work you've done for a damned long time.'

'It could easily be that and still not be up to much,' said

Penderel. 'But I know what you mean. And I can't help feeling——'

But there came an interruption from Gladys, who was still standing near the foot of the stairs. 'I can hear somebody talking up there,' she called to them.

Penderel moved a step or two in her direction. 'That'll be the Wavertons. They must be introspecting together on one of the upper floors, walking up and down corridors still playing Truth. And quite right too!'

Her hand went up. 'Hush! I'm trying to listen. They're coming down, I think. Oh! what's that?' They had all heard it—a kind of laugh. And now the Wavertons came running downstairs, pale and dusty and somehow rather tattered.

'Listen, you fellows.' Philip hurried across to the two men, and began to gasp out his news.

'What is it?' Gladys clutched at Margaret. 'Tell me quick.' Something terrible was going to happen, she knew there was. She felt sick. Everything was suddenly falling to pieces.

'There's a madman upstairs,' Margaret cried jerkily. 'Morgan's let him out. He's dangerous. They both are.'

'Where's he now?' She knew, knew there was something, had known it all along.

'Up there, somewhere.' Margaret made a little gesture of helplessness. 'Coming down, perhaps.'

'We must all get out of the way then. Lock ourselves in somewhere.'

'He might set fire to the place. He's tried to do that before.'

'They can prevent him. Three of them.' Gladys looked towards the men, and then, moved by a common impulse, they both hurried across. They felt the whole house pressing down upon them.

'Even if he's as bad as all that,' Sir William was saying, 'the three of us can down him.' He was quite cool, and evidently— rather to their surprise—a man of courage. But then no imagination was harrying him. He didn't see the whole fabric of sense and security shredding, rotting away.

'But there's Morgan; don't forget him,' Philip replied. 'I've had a tussle with him already and was lucky enough to trip him. He was a bit slow and silly, of course. But he's as strong as a bull. I don't know what sort of state he's in now, but he might be as bad as the lunatic—worse.'

'If the worst came to the worst,' Sir William said, 'we could all clear out. In fact the best thing we can do is to get out of the way.'

'You're forgetting what Waverton said,' Penderel put in. 'I mean about him setting fire to things. This old place'd burn easily, wouldn't it?' He looked at Philip.

'I should think it would. It's full of rotten old timber. That's the danger. If he gets down here, left to himself, he could set the whole place going in a jiffy.'

'Well, let him, I say,' said Gladys, viciously. 'Let the rotten old place burn.'

'No, that's mad, Gladys,' Penderel told her.

'Besides,' Philip added hastily, 'there are the other Femms——'

'Poor old Sir Roderick upstairs, unable to move,' cried Margaret. 'It was he who warned us, only just in time too. We can't leave him.'

Philip and Penderel hastened to agree. Sir William looked at them and then at the stairs. 'Well, what are we going to do, then?' he asked. 'Time's going. Though nothing's happened yet. It may be all piffle. All these people here are a bit crazy, so far as I can see.'

'No, it isn't.' Margaret was vehement. 'Didn't you hear that horrible laugh? And Philip saw the room.'

Gladys wrung her hands. 'I'm sure it's true; I know it is.' She sought out Penderel with hollowed eyes. 'Yes, I do. I've felt it creeping.' Then she recovered herself. 'But we can do something, can't we?' It was addressed to him alone, wistfully; the others were nothing.

'Of course we can,' he told her. But he felt a sudden ache, and there followed closely upon it a growing anger.

Then they all jumped. A door had been opened, and someone was standing there. It was Miss Femm. How she came to be there, nobody could imagine, but there she was, still fully dressed, peering at them over a stump of candle. They didn't wait for her to screech out a question. 'Your brother's loose!' cried Philip, who was nearest.

'What, Saul?' The name went screaming up.

'They're coming down now. Look!' Gladys cried, pointing. A dark bulk was moving slowly down the stairs, and another behind it, with a vague blur of face turned towards them. The one behind must be Saul. That hand sliding down the banisters was Saul's. Now it had stopped; but Morgan was still moving, coming down alone.

'Don't do anything yet,' Philip whispered. 'Morgan may be all right now. We'll see.'

Morgan reached the bottom, lurched forward a step or two, and then stood still, lowering at them. Such light as there was from the little lamp fell now on his face, which looked horrible—for it was all covered with blood. His hands too seemed to be reddened.

'Cut himself with that glass,' Philip whispered again.

'What's he going to do?' This was from Penderel, though he was not looking at Morgan but at that hand which still rested on the banisters.

'Get back.' Sir William was motioning to Margaret and Gladys.

Miss Femm had been standing absolutely still, staring fixedly at Morgan. Now she shook her fist at him, and her voice went piercing through them all. 'Morgan, you brute beast, go away. Hide yourself before God strikes you dead.'

The laugh they had heard before, empty and terrible, rang down from the dim stairs. 'That's Rebecca, sister Rebecca. Don't listen to her, Morgan. She's been talking to God for years now and He's never heard her once. He thinks she's a maggot, a fat little white maggot. He doesn't know she's got a soul. She'll have to die and be born again before He'll hear her. They're all maggots—still creeping in the rotting old corpse they call life.' Saul's voice thickened with sudden fury. 'Trample 'em, smash 'em—and then I'll burn their filthy pulp—leave nothing but ashes—clean ashes—clean, clean, clean!' After that it was a foul gabble. They had a moment's vision of a white and blindly working face, pushed out over the banisters into the light, while the voice went gibbering on.

Then there was a little space of silence, during which nobody moved. But it seemed to them as if the ground beneath their feet was sinking, as if they were blackly descending through putrid air.

Now the madman on the stairs spoke again and his mood had suddenly changed; he seemed quietly merry. 'No, Morgan, old flesh and bone, wait, wait for me.' They saw the hand disappear. 'Still something yet to do. Then we'll finish it together.' A stir in the shadows, a creak or two from the stairs, and he was gone.

Instead of waiting, however, Morgan, who had been standing there, glowering at Philip, was suddenly quickened into life. With a hoarse cry, he charged across, straight at Philip, like a mastodon. There was just time for Philip to swing aside and escape the full weight of the charge, and the next moment they were all struggling together. Sir William was hanging on to one great arm and shoulder, and Philip on to the other.

'Get him in there,' screamed Miss Femm, as they went desperately swaying. 'You can shut him up.' She was pointing to the door through which she had come.

Penderel made up his mind now, and there was no time to be lost. He threw himself at Morgan, who went rolling back with the other two still clinging to him. 'Can you do that?' he cried to them, as he pushed at the struggling giant. 'Shall I knock him on the head?'

'We'll manage,' Philip gasped. They were now near the door, which Miss Femm had flung wide open. A tremendous heave of Morgan's right arm sent Philip flying back, but he quickly recovered himself and sent his fist, with all his weight behind it, crashing into Morgan's face. The man spun round, sending Sir William, pale now and dripping with sweat but still game, banging into the doorway. Philip grabbed at the loose arm and savagely twisted it behind its owner's back, at the same time charging forward. 'Rush him down the corridor,' he cried to Sir William. They disappeared through the doorway, into the dark.

Miss Femm stood there, holding the door with one hand and her lighted candle held high in the other. 'Come on, you,' she screeched at Margaret and Gladys. 'In here with me.'

Margaret, who had faltered forward, looked at her with horror and could not find her voice.

'No, no!' Gladys cried, looking from her to Penderel.

Miss Femm stepped back. 'Then stay there. Sluts!' she yelled. She banged the door behind her and they heard her lock it.

Margaret ran forward, crying, 'She's locked it. And Philip's there, Philip!' Her hands were fumbling at the door now.

'It's done now. Come away.' Penderel was at her side, though his eyes were on Gladys.

'But Philip's in there, with that man,' she cried again. Then she turned on him, with a flash of scorn: 'And what are you going to do?'

'I'm going to wait here—for the other man,' he told them very quietly.

Gladys was clutching his arm. 'No, no, you can't. Come away.'

'Listen, there's no time to waste,' he said, and as he spoke he hustled them across the room. 'I must wait here until they've got Morgan safely tucked away. He may be down any moment. And you've got to be out of the way.'

'I'll stay,' Gladys cried chokingly.

'You can't, my dear,' he told her. 'And we must hurry.'

They were at the other side of the room now. 'But where can we go?' Margaret was asking, looking at him piteously.

'In there.' He pointed to the door that he had opened before, when he had been changing his clothes. He remembered that there was a key on the inside. Now he ran forward, took it out, and then swept them in, Margaret first. For one brief moment his arm was round Gladys. 'Sorry there's no light for you. Yes, there is, though.' He rushed away and then returned carrying the candle that Philip had had, now guttering sadly, and thrust it into Gladys's hand. 'You'll be all right in there.' His eyes dwelt on her face as if he was trying to remember it for ever. 'Quite all right. Cheerio!'

Before they could do or say anything more he had closed the door and locked them in, leaving the key in the lock. If he left them free to rush out, anything might happen. He walked very slowly and quietly back into the middle of the hall, looking up at the stairs and listening.

CHAPTER XIII

Time stood still for Penderel, waiting there in the hall. A few moments before, when he had been hustling the women across to that room, it had seemed as if there wasn't a second to waste, but now, as he listened in loneliness between those locked doors, he found there was time enough and to spare. No sound came from above. He crossed over to the door through which Morgan and Waverton and Sir William had disappeared in a struggling mass, and he tried the handle. It was locked, of course; he knew very well it was. That meant that Waverton and Sir William would first have to dispose of Morgan and then get the key from the Femm woman, before they could join him. And Morgan might easily be a match for both of them for some time yet. He listened at the door. Vague, distant sounds came through, suggesting that Morgan had not yet been overpowered but was still putting up a fight somewhere at the end of the corridor, perhaps in or near the kitchen. A creak from the stairs sent him back into the middle of the hall, with his heart-beats filling his ears. But nobody was there.

If that had been the moment for action, he felt, all would have been well. There was, however, nothing to do but wait, listen to the mocking old timbers and wait, stare at the jumping shadows and wait; and now he suddenly felt sick and afraid. He wanted to run away, to take the good the night had brought him, out of its darkness, and hurry with it into safety. But he could not take it away, for if he went now, hiding his head, it would not go with him: all would be lost. Well, he had wanted something to do, and here was something to do. He hadn't had to wait long, he told himself grimly. How queer it was that there was something inside you that could relish, grinning with irony, the most damnable situation you found yourself in, pointing out how damnable it was! He'd discovered that in France, when, as now, something in him was afraid and something else wasn't, something shook and something grinned. Some of the old faces came popping up, smiled, and were gone; fellows he thought he'd forgotten; a spectral parade; and he wanted to keep one steadily before him so that he could cry 'It's a good war' and once again hear it call back to him, just one of the daft old slogans: 'Jam for the troops, mate.' He would feel better after that. He might give Gladys a shout. She'd understand. But no, that wouldn't do.

His eye went travelling idly up the dimly lighted stairs, waiting for madness to creep down from the dark, and then suddenly his mind cleared. His place wasn't here, dithering and dreaming, but at the top of those stairs. Once down here, the madman might easily escape him and let hell loose, unless of course the other two came back before he arrived. So long as there wasn't another way down, the best place for him was obviously at the top there; and even if there should be another way down, he wouldn't be much worse off up there, because it wouldn't take him long to get back again. And the sooner he went up the better.

He walked forward, then stopped and looked round hesitantly. His hand went to his forehead, which was cold and wet. Wasn't there something he could take with him, something to grip? Well, there was a poker, and that was better than nothing. Hastily he seized it, and was crossing to the foot of the stairs when he bethought himself of the light. He couldn't take it with him, that would be too dangerous; but if he put the lamp somewhere near the front door it would throw a little more light on the place where he would have to take his stand, at the very top of the stairs.

He crept up, slowly, shakily, his shadow leaping and sprawling before him. There were little noises everywhere now, not a stair in the house without its creak. All that part of the house that yawned above him seemed tense, expectant. The little patch of darkness at the top was thick and crawling with unrevealed terrors. A step or two more and out of that blackness would spring a white, gibbering face. He'd had a dream like that once—it all came back to him, raw and palpitating, the whole experience, almost between one stair and the next—and he remembered how he had wakened, a little boy sobbing in the night, to find his mother bending over him. Who would bend over him now? Why hadn't they turned God into this vast maternal presence, smooth hands and a murmuring voice and a familiar lovely smell in the dark?

He was standing at the very top now, one hand behind him, touching the rail, the other achingly folded round the poker. While his eyes stared into the shadows and his ears seemed to run on and search the landing, his thoughts went sickeningly racing round. He was terribly afraid now, angry with himself for standing there. Why shouldn't he rush downstairs, join Gladys in that room and lock the door, or plunge out into the night itself, into safety and sweet air? However, probably nothing would happen. But then, if nothing happened, he would be all right here. And if he went and something did happen, whether it hurt him or not, he knew that all would be over, the road missed for ever; the rest would be just breathing and eating and sleeping, with his spirit, a poor shamed ghost, returning time and again to take its stand on these stairs.

Yes, he could only stay. What was that? Surely that was somebody moving, not very far away? Why didn't Waverton and Porterhouse show themselves? But then they wouldn't, not because they didn't want to, but because it always happened like that: he might have known that he would have to be alone. He'd always been more afraid of madness than anything else—the very thought of a maniac had always filled him with terror, and when this creature had raved on the stairs he'd felt sick, as if he were being pelted with lumps of putrid flesh—and of course he'd have to come in the end to face it alone. The thing came at last, the darkness shaping itself, and immediately everybody disappeared, doors were locked all round you, and you found yourself alone with it. That noise again, much nearer this time! Yes, he was at the other end of the landing. He was coming on steadily.

'Stop!' he cried, quite involuntarily. 'Stay there, d'you hear? Don't try to get past. I've got a poker here and I shall use it.' His voice was ridiculously hoarse and shaky, not at all commanding.

The footsteps ceased, and he found he could just see a vague outline of the madman standing there a few yards away. Undoubtedly he had stopped at the sound of a voice, but he made no reply. Penderel waited and then asked himself despairingly how he could have expected a reply. Madness wouldn't stand there bandying words with him. Nevertheless he had stopped.

'Go back and don't be a fool.' Sheer necessity compelled him to speak out again, for only the sound of his own voice kept him from running away. 'You're not coming past here. Get back at once.' It was woefully grotesque and futile perhaps, yet it raised his spirits a little.

Now there came an answering gabble from that vague shape, a gabble that seemed to end in a kind of chuckle. There was a movement, followed by a quick pattering down the landing. He was going away.

In his astonishment and relief, Penderel sank back against the banisters. Was it all over, then? Had he really gone? Did it only need a command or two, however shaky, just simple courage, no matter if it was raised perilously on tip-toe, to turn aside—flicking it away—what had seemed doom itself? There came now a moment of triumph, and his spirits went soaring. It seemed as if the corner were turned at last, and he had a flashing vision of life stretched widely and gloriously before him, the shining happy valley, lost for years and apparently gone for ever, a dream bitterly cast off, until this strange night brought glimpse after glimpse of it through thinning mist, and now finally swung it into full view. Now he knew what it was to be alive. He could have cried aloud with happiness.

The very next moment he was sick at heart. He heard the

quick pattering again; the footsteps were hastening towards
him through the darkness; and everything, even his courage,
collapsed at the sound. He wanted to run headlong now, to
run crying defeat and then to hide himself for ever. But one
last slender cord of will, still unbroken, kept him standing
there.

'Stop!' he cried again. But how feeble it sounded! He wanted
to implore now and not to command.

The maniac had stopped already, however, though this time
he was nearer. There burst from him a sudden yell of rage.

Penderel drew himself up and tried to control his voice.
'You can't come here, I tell you——' he began; but before he
could say any more, something heavy, a chair or a small table,
came flying through the air, smashing against his right arm
and ribs, sending the poker clattering below, and knocking
him sideways and backwards against the banisters as it crashed
into them itself. He fell down, helpless in a spinning world,
dizzy and sick. His arm hurt dreadfully, seemed to be broken.
Soon the creature would be trampling the life out of him. He
tried to rise, but it was too late, the maniac was upon him, and
he received a blow in the face that sent his head back with a
dreadful jolt and blinded him for a moment.

There was no fear left in him now. In an agony of effort he
flung himself forward, grabbed the man's legs and put out all
his strength in one great lift. Down he came, and now they
were rolling about the floor, tearing at one another. Penderel
found himself possessed by a tremendous fury: 'You bloody
swine!' he was jerking out, 'I'll kill you.' He contrived to
scramble to his feet, but before he had time to do anything
but pull himself up, dizzily and achingly, the other was on his
feet too and renewing the attack. He was a much older man
than Penderel, but he was also much bigger and heavier and
seemed to be unusually powerful.

Penderel had his back against the banisters. For a minute
or two, while the madman was still breathless, there was little
danger. He was able to dodge or ward off the lumbering blows

aimed at him. He covered himself with his left arm, for the right, though not entirely useless, hurt him terribly every time he moved it. Indeed, all his right side ached, and whenever he took a deep breath he felt a little stab of pain there. Standing where he was, he wasn't really barring the way downstairs, though he could leap upon the man's back if he should try to go down; but it was evident now that Saul Femm—Penderel had begun to give him his name—intended to settle with him before going any further. And if he could only hold out here, he told himself, the others would be in little danger. Waverton and Porterhouse might return any minute now, and even if he was finished before they did return, he would leave Saul in no condition to deal with them. There was just a minute or two in which to think of these things.

Now Saul was completely recovered and, screaming wildly, he hurled himself upon Penderel, who heard the banisters cracking ominously behind him. He felt helpless in the man's grasp. The pressure of the banisters against the small of his back was agonising. And struggle as he might, he could not release himself. One hand was fumbling for his throat. The banisters were cracking again, and he felt himself being lifted. Desperately he drew up one leg and, hanging on with all his might, drove his knee into the other man's belly, released the pressure a little, contrived to slip his leg down again, pushed a hand up under Saul's slavering chin, and by summoning the very remnant of his strength was able to send them both tottering forward a pace, clear of the banisters. There they swayed, six inches this way and that, at close grips.

Blood and sweat ran down his face, blinding him; the pain in his side was intolerable; and he felt his strength ebbing out; but he held on, held on as if there was nothing else left in the world to do. And all the while his mind, escaping from this shameful nightmare of stench and blood and pain, went darting back to queer memories and flashing along the edge of vivid little dreams; and once more he was lying in the long cool grass near the playing-field wall, or listening to Jim and

Tom Ranger outside a tent, a glimmer of starlight there, or standing under the blossom at Garthstead; and oddly mingling with these memories were thoughts that came and went like swallows, thoughts of the dusk and glitter of town at early evening, quiet pipes in the night, the loud jolly orchestra and the brightening curtain, that little place up five flights of stairs, Gladys laughing at him, brave eyes meeting his through a door suddenly opened. They were so long, so long swaying there in the dark, there was time for a whole shadow show of life.

He couldn't see at all now; he had to fight for each stabbing breath; and the blood drummed relentlessly in his ears. One hand had found Saul's throat and tightened on it, but he could no longer hold his ground and fell back inch after inch until at last he seemed to be lifted off his feet. He went crashing against the banisters; something was breaking; the life was being squeezed out of him; but still he held on. Now they were clear of the banisters again, for Saul had relaxed his pressure for a moment and had been compelled to fall back a step, with Penderel still clinging to him. Saul put out all his remaining strength in one tremendous heave. 'I'm done, I'm done,' Penderel was crying, crying through a black night of crashing, splintering woodwork and rushing air. And then there was no more pain.

CHAPTER XIV

Margaret was trying the handle of the door. 'He's locked it,' she cried, staring at Gladys.

'I know he has.' Gladys had sunk to her knees. She put the candlestick, with its feeble, spluttering flame on the floor beside her, and stretched out a hand to the door, leaning against it. 'He's shut us in because he thought we'd be safe in here.' She spoke slowly, dully.

'I don't want to be safe, to be shut in like this.' Margaret rattled the handle uselessly. 'I want to know what's happening. I want to be with Phil—my husband.'

'Don't you see?' Gladys had roused herself and was looking up now, her eyes bright with resentment. 'He's out there, waiting for that lunatic to come down, and shoved us in here to be out of the way. You don't seem to understand what he's doing. You thought he was dodging it, didn't you? My God!'

'I did at first,' Margaret said gently. 'I'm sorry.' And as she looked down at the girl's pale face, working queerly in that jumpy little light, she felt sorry too, sorry for her, sorry for everybody.

'As if he would!' Then her tone changed from indignation to bitterness. 'Well, I wish to God he had, wish we'd never come back. It would have to be him, of course it would be. It was just waiting for him. That's silly, I suppose. I don't care. I'm all to pieces now—and he's out there, as lonely as hell, waiting for that—that thing.'

'It'll be all right,' Margaret told her, trying to keep her voice quiet and confident. 'The others will be back soon. Then there'll be three of them.'

'That woman locked the other door,' Gladys muttered.

'They'll get the key from her when they've done with Morgan,' Margaret went on. But she was thinking how all this crazy locking of doors made it seem like a bad dream. She glanced round in the dying light and shivered. 'Where are we?'

'I don't know. What does it matter?' Gladys raised herself up and tried to listen through the door.

Margaret took up the candlestick and moved forward a few paces. She saw nothing but the dimmest shapes of furniture, however, for the little spluttering flame gave a last jump, trembled, and then rapidly dwindled. Her spirits sank with it as the darkness closed round her. She trailed back to the door and, when the last flicker had gone, she let the candlestick fall to the ground. 'What's happening?' She bent forward.

'Oh, I can't hear a thing,' Gladys whispered.

Together they listened at the door, and it seemed to be hours before they heard anything but their own quick breathing and heart-beats. They were lost in a pulsating darkness.

'We can't do anything but wait,' whispered Margaret at last. Somehow she daren't raise her voice above a whisper.

'I can hear him moving about now; can you?' Gladys listened again. 'Bill and your husband don't seem to have come out yet. I believe he's going upstairs.'

'Yes, he is,' Margaret told her, and could feel her trembling. There was a long pause, during which they listened again, then Margaret went on: 'I can't hear anything now. Perhaps he's waiting at the top. That's horrible, isn't it? Why doesn't Philip come back? It's awful waiting here.'

'It's worse waiting there,' cried Gladys, raising her voice now. 'With that ghastly loony creeping down. Oh, my God!' She cleared her throat. 'I expect you know what's the matter with me, or you must think I'm going mad too.'

'I feel we're all going mad to-night,' Margaret broke in, hastily. 'Everything's turned crazy and horrible. That's the awful thing, isn't it?—that you can't trust anything, like being in a nightmare. Haven't you been feeling that?'

'Yes, I have.' Gladys was at once eager and piteous. 'Didn't I tell you before? I knew, I knew. Something told me all along, and I tried to tell him but I couldn't make him understand. It was only a feeling—but you know what I mean?'

'Who did you try to tell?'

'Penderel, of course. When we were outside. That's what I was going to tell you, I mean when I said you'd know what's the matter with me—because, you see—Oh, you know—I love him. We can talk now, can't we? Yes, we went outside and sat and talked, and then I found it out; came as quick as lightning, sudden but absolutely dead certain.' Then she added, simply: 'And you know what it means. You're in love with your husband, aren't you?'

'Yes, I am.' This was neither the time nor the place, Margaret felt, for all those delicate reservations that her truthful mind had so often brought out and examined. Then she realised, in a flash, that they no longer appeared to exist. She couldn't remember what they were. And she didn't want to remember. 'I haven't always thought so,' she went on. 'But I am.'

'I knew you were,' Gladys whispered. 'I could tell, always can. But I suppose it doesn't make you ache any more, does it?'

'I think,' said Margaret, slowly, 'it's beginning to, again.'

'It's funny it's so different——' Gladys began, but then broke off. There was a crash outside. 'My God! Did you hear that? And we can't do a thing! Has that lunatic come down, do you think? Are they fighting?'

'I think they must be. It's horrible, horrible.'

'And he's there by himself. The other two haven't come back. Why don't they come?' Gladys pressed her hands together in the darkness.

'I don't know,' Margaret stammered. 'Something may have happened to them. That beast—Morgan—and Miss Femm.' Then something seemed to snap inside her. 'Oh, I can't bear it, can't bear it any longer.' Her legs crumpled like paper and she slipped down the door, sobbing.

Gladys was kneeling by her side now, with an arm about her. 'Never mind, never mind, Mrs. Waverton. It's awful, isn't it, but it'll all come right for you, you'll see. Nothing'll have happened to him. Your man can look after himself.' They clung together, while through the dark, from behind the door, came tiny vague sounds, a mysterious thud-thudding. But neither of them wanted to listen any longer. They could only wait, comforting one another, until the door was opened again, to reveal their fate. Until that moment arrived, this was all their world, and they could only cling together in the darkness and cry to one another their hope and their despair.

'It's worn me down,' said Margaret, brokenly. 'You've no idea what it's been like, for me, here. One thing after another. First, Miss Femm—telling me about her sister—then touching me—and that horrible room of hers. Then Morgan—he came after me—like a beast. And Philip had to fight him, upstairs. And then that strange old man—lying so still in his bed— whispering terrible things. And now this. All going on and on. Everything strange and dark and getting queerer and darker. No end to it. Until at last you begin to feel that all the safe and clean and sane things have gone for ever. You can't hold on for ever. It's been different for you perhaps; but don't you see what I mean?'

Gladys murmured that she did and tightened her clasp. She didn't understand it all, but that didn't matter. Nothing mattered now except keeping close until that door opened.

'I hated it at first,' Margaret went on. 'But then when we were talking round the table I liked it. And I thought Philip and I could easily find one another after that, because it seemed so easy to know and understand people, even strangers, so easy to be happy with someone you once loved.'

'I felt that too, or something like it.' Gladys was crying very quietly. 'Oh, what am I crying for! It doesn't matter though. But—it was better than that with me. It was really beginning, see? First, listening to all of you, then talking about myself. Then talking to him out there. And being able to laugh about everything together, and knowing as well that I could do a lot for him. He was absolutely fed up, didn't care a damn about anything. And I was like that really. And then I thought, if it lasted, I wouldn't be lonely any more, wouldn't be going in at night sometimes wishing I was dead. And even if it didn't last, I'd had something, you see, something different. . . .'

Margaret had been mechanically telling herself that it was all very sudden and strange, this love affair of her companion's. But when Gladys's voice trailed away, there came, flowing up through the silence, the thought that it was not strange at all, that it was as simple and natural as the breath in their bodies. Now it seemed strange that people whose hearts were empty could meet on such a night and talk through this darkness without loving. 'I see,' she said, after a long pause. Then she added: 'You know, I didn't like you at first, but I do now.'

'I hated you,' said Gladys, very close and warm. 'But that's gone completely.' She thought for a moment. 'I don't think I hated you really. I was frightened.'

'Frightened?' As soon as the word was out, however, Margaret realised what Gladys had meant. She too had been frightened of Penderel, alarmed by something unharnessed, mocking, anarchic in him that had called to its brother, usually safely hidden away, in Philip; and so she had decided that she detested him. And so people crept about, absurdly frightened of one another, pretending to hate, keeping it up even when they had to take shelter together in such a place as this.

'Yes, I was frightened really,' Gladys was whispering, 'of the way you walked and talked and were dressed. I felt you despised me. But now it's all right, isn't it? Aren't we women silly with one another? As if there wasn't enough——!'

There was a little silence between them, and Margaret's mind returned to the world outside. 'I can hear little noises all the time,' she said, at last. 'I feel sure something's happening there. What's that?'

It was a kind of cracking sound, and they heard it repeated several times. Then it stopped and they could only catch the noises they had heard before. At last there came another crack, louder this time, and it seemed to them, as they listened, trembling in the dark, as if something were breaking.

'What is it? What's happening?' Gladys cried. 'My God, I can't stand much more of this!' Then her voice rose to a shriek. 'Oh, what's that?'

The crash and splintering and heavy thud-thud still rang in their ears. They clung to one another in agony of apprehension. The moments passed, but there came no other sound. The silence, as if heavy with doom, weighed down upon them.

'What was it?' The words came from Margaret in a hollow whisper, like ghost talking to ghost.

Gladys gave a choking little cry and Margaret felt the girl's whole body relax and droop. For a few moments she remained passive, but then suddenly she sprang up and fell on the door in a fury, battering at it with her fists and even kicking it. The next minute her strength had left her and she was in Margaret's arms, quietly sobbing. Holding her tight and murmuring over her as if she were a child, Margaret was now the comforter and immediately felt better. We're being child and grown-up in turn, she was thinking; and if we always worked like that, we could all comfort one another through anything.

Gladys was quiet now. At last she spoke, but it was only as if an odd thought here and there were slipping into words. 'We said we'd have a little flat, somewhere high up, very little and cheap. . . . You wouldn't think that much fun, I suppose?'

'We had one once,' Margaret told her, gently, 'when we first began, and we thought it fun.'

'I shouldn't have been able to do much at first, but I'd have managed. I'd have liked that. I told him so. Even the little rows would have been a kind of fun. You understand, don't you?'

Margaret found that she couldn't reply.

'There's a lot of fun in life, isn't there?' Gladys went on, very slowly, as if she were talking in her sleep. 'I've had some. But not lately. Somehow if you start missing it, you go on missing it. And it's so easy to get right off the track of it, just lose the way. We'd missed it, but we'd have found it together. I would anyhow . . .'

'Oh, why are you talking like that?' Margaret cried. 'I can't bear it. You sound—I don't know—as if something's broken—in you, I mean.'

'I felt as if it had,' said Gladys, 'when something broke out there. You heard it.'

'No, no.' Margaret was desperate. 'That's all nonsense. Rouse yourself. We don't really know what's happened. It's only waiting here, in the dark, not knowing anything, that's wearing us down. If we give in, I don't know what will happen. We can't let these things drive us out of our senses, beat us down. That's what they're trying to do. We won't have it, will we? Let's do something. Bang on the door again.'

'I did that,' said Gladys, dully. 'There's nobody to let us out.'

'Oh, don't say that! It sounds so horrible.' And Margaret began pounding on the door. Then she stopped herself. 'Perhaps we shouldn't, though,' she faltered. She thought of that vague, gibbering figure on the stairs. Suppose he was at the other side of the door, alone, heard them knocking and opened it. Her hands fell helplessly to her side, and once more she saw life trembling on the edge of a pit, with unreason darkening the sky above it. If Philip didn't come, it wouldn't be long before she would be absolutely beaten down and everything would be lost.

Gladys stirred. 'I thought I heard something then. Yes, there you are. Voices.'

'I can hear Philip,' Margaret broke in, jubilantly. 'I'm sure I can.' Without thinking now, she rapped on the door. Then she stopped to listen again. 'Yes, it is Philip. It's all right now. I'm sure it is.' She called out and rapped again.

'Hello!' Philip was very close now, just at the other side of the door. 'Is that you, Margaret?'

'Yes, here we are,' she called back. 'Let us out, Philip. Isn't the key there?'

'Yes it is. You're all right, aren't you?' His voice sounded queer. 'Well, wait a few minutes.'

'We can't wait. What's the matter?' But he had gone, and they were left to listen and wonder and whisper together a little longer in the darkness.

'I'm frightened, I'm frightened,' said Gladys at last, putting out a hand and coming close again.

'So am I,' replied Margaret. 'But it's really all right now, Gladys, isn't it?'

'I don't know,' she whispered. 'I don't know.'

Then they waited in silence for the door to open.

CHAPTER XV

It had seemed as if dawn were postponed for ever, yet it came at last. Philip noticed a vague trouble in the air and then a faint greying of things. He alone appeared to be awake now. He was sitting in a chair, and his arms were around Margaret, who was leaning against him, curled across another and lower chair. For some time he had been sitting there, quiet, unstirring, numbed, but with his thoughts going on and on, like a river flowing through a frozen land. He seemed to have been there a long time now. Already the events of the night had receded; the struggle with Morgan in the hall here, along the corridor, in the kitchen, and the final victory that sent him, cowed, beaten, into the cellar; the fantastic interview with Miss Femm, who would not surrender the key of the door into the hall at first and had to be stormed at; the discovery of the lifeless bodies of Penderel and Saul Femm, one with his neck broken and the other mysteriously killed, perhaps from shock and a weak heart; the huddling away of the bodies, the scenes that followed with Margaret and Gladys and the two Femms; already these events were receding, a haze was creeping over them, though the tale was hardly three hours old.

He himself had not slept, though there was something hot and aching about his eyes and a weight upon their lids. He had been busy making Margaret comfortable, holding her securely, and now she slept. Not far away, Sir William, who had long been exhausted and had not easily recovered from the blow that Morgan had given him, was stretched out in the other armchair, dozing heavily. The rich baronet, Philip reflected, had come out of it all extraordinarily well. Brigand he might be, but he was certainly a man. He had shown courage and nerve during the fight with Morgan and later, and, what was even more surprising, he had been magnificent with Gladys afterwards, the 'lass,' as he had called her with a gruff tenderness that seemed to be part of the real North-country self he usually kept hidden away.

Philip watched the grey light steal into the room and then begin to creep towards every corner. There was Gladys, the most tragic figure among them. She was half-sitting, half-lying on the floor, with her head against Sir William's knee and one arm flung across it. She, too, was sleeping peacefully at last, completely worn out after her long storm of sobbing. When she had first learned of Penderel's death, she had been strangely quiet; and it was only afterwards, when in spite of all they could say to dissuade her she had gone to look at his body and had suddenly flung herself down upon it, that she had lost all her self-control. And now she was asleep, and when she wakened to the world again the night's tragedy would have lost something of its stabbing power, would already be a memory, be softened, gauzed about with dream, and she would be ready to go quietly away, to complete—and how strange that seemed—her journey.

His thoughts wandered on as he watched the room tremble between darkness and light. Penderel and poor crazed Saul Femm had only seemed to be sleeping, as if suddenly weary of their long wrestling bout, when they had found them, twisted on the floor beneath the broken banisters. And there had seemed, he remembered, to be a queer brotherhood between them. You felt they were going to awaken somewhere else and immediately shake hands and talk it all out together.

Margaret stirred and his arm tightened about her, but she didn't waken. Nothing much had happened between them; they hadn't had it out in the old cool and clever way; but they had exchanged a glance or two, a few broken sentences; and it looked as if everything might be different yet. 'I'm so lonely,' she had whispered once; and then: 'It's unbearable without love.' But that was in the last long terror of the dark, and perhaps he ought to forget it now. Still, the sun would set again, and the darkness would come again. And he had said once, when she was burying her face in his coat: 'Let's make another start'; and he had felt an answering grip upon his arm. But the real moment which might change everything for them, had been one of silence, just a clasp of hands. That was when they were standing together on the landing upstairs. Mr. Femm had come and gone like a shaking ghost; Miss Femm had departed to pray by the body of her dead brother; Gladys, growing calmer at last, had been handed over to Sir William; and it was then they had remembered old Sir Roderick upstairs, lying there wondering and helpless in the dark. Nobody could have visited him because Philip himself still had the key. Together they had returned there, haunted by a curiously poignant memory of that room, that last little outpost of sanity, and together they had crept in, carrying the remaining inch of lighted candle, to whisper the end of the story to him who had begun it for them in a whisper or two. It was a strange errand, with a conclusion stranger still. Not a sound nor a movement had come from that shadowy bed, and when they crept forward to look at the old man, it had seemed as if he too had died. Then they had noticed his faint breathing, the very lightest sigh of life, and had seen that he was calmly sleeping. Probably he had slept through everything. They left him undisturbed, but when they had closed the door behind them, they stood very close together, in silence, and hand had reached out for hand. Something had united them at that moment, little more than a breath perhaps, and yet it brought them so close, so close. Surely they could begin again now?

Somebody moved and grunted. That was Sir William. 'Hello!' Philip called softly. 'You awake?'

'Yes, worse luck,' Sir William replied, in a very hoarse, uncertain voice. 'Can't either sleep or keep awake. I'm sore all over. Keep thinking, too.'

'So do I,' said Philip, companionably, and then waited.

'Tell you what keeps coming into my mind,' the other went on, after a pause. 'Remember when we took hold of that poor devil, the lunatic? Well, I noticed something lying on the floor on my side, just by his coat. It was a couple of cards. I can tell you what they were. Seven of clubs and five of diamonds. I shan't ever forget 'em either. Seven of clubs and five of diamonds. And then some more came tumbling out of his pocket when we lifted the body. He'd a pack in his pocket. Must have played patience up there sometimes, poor devil. That got me somehow. Don't know how it is, but can't forget those cards.'

Philip made a little answering noise that showed he was listening, but said nothing. He hoped Sir William would go on talking, but he didn't much want to talk himself. There was silence for a few minutes.

'I liked that lad Penderel, you know,' Sir William remarked at last, as if musing aloud. 'He wasn't my sort and I don't suppose he liked me, but I liked him. I'd have done something for him too. He was going to get a job, you know. About the last thing he talked about.'

'What was he going to do?' Philip found he could talk about Penderel quite calmly now.

'God knows! He probably wouldn't have done it long, whatever it was. He'd got guts all right—we know that—and I fancy he'd brains, but I don't see him fitting in anywhere, I mean I didn't see him. You never know, of course, you never know. But this is no way to talk about the poor lad, is it? I liked him, liked him from the first, when he was talking about himself. I thought it seemed damned unfair, somehow. I dunno. What can you do? And it seems a damned sight worse now. Won't bear thinking about, will it? Gladys here's sleeping like a three-year-old now. Well, I'll see she's all right. Made up my mind about that.'

Then Sir William struggled with a series of yawns. 'Nearly dead for want of sleep,' he confessed. 'How about you? But then you're still young. I'm getting on, and if I didn't know it before, I know it now.' He yawned again. 'There'll be something to do about this business. Just thought of that. Inquests and God knows what else, keeping us dodging about for days. Damned nuisance, eh? Lot to do to-morrow—to-day I mean—if we're not still cut off. Well, we'll have to get busy. But must have some sleep first.' His voice sank to a mere grunt and in another minute he had dozed off again.

Daylight itself was at the windows, suddenly chilling the place. Philip shivered a little, feeling cold now and very hungry. The arm that held Margaret was cramped and aching and very gently he tried to move it. She stirred, turned her head, and he saw that her eyes were wide open though still vague with sleep. Something caught at his heart as he stared down at her face, for she looked different, at once dreamy and curiously fragile, yet he remembered her looking like that once before. Was it when Betty was born?

For some little time she remained like that, and neither stirred again nor spoke. He leaned forward and watched her eyes clear themselves of sleep and then slowly move this way and that, up to his face, towards the windows. 'It's nearly daylight,' she said at last, very softly.

'Yes, it's dawn,' he told her. 'I've been watching it arrive.' He saw her eyes close again and waited a moment. Then he added: 'It's been a long time coming.'

Her only reply was a little murmuring sound from her closed lips. It seemed as if she were falling asleep again. The next moment, however, her eyes were wide open once more and looked up at him. 'You've not been asleep, Phil, have you?' she said.

'Not yet. I suppose I've been thinking in a numbed sort of fashion. I must say I'm tired.'

'You look tired,' she whispered. 'Try to go to sleep. Don't bother about anything any more.' Her eyes closed again, but she raised her head a little and he bent forward and kissed her, very gently.

Now holding her lightly at arms length, he half raised himself from the chair and gingerly tried his legs. 'I'm horribly cramped,' he said softly. 'You must be too. Try this big chair while I work this stiffness off.' She nodded, and he moved to one side and helped her into the arm-chair.

'Is Gladys asleep?' she whispered.

'Yes; she's never moved.'

'I'm glad. We mustn't waken her.' She sank back and he bent over her and seemed to see her eyes cloud over with sleep again.

'I think I'll go over to the window,' he remarked, 'just to see what it's like outside.'

She looked at him and tried to smile. 'It's different now, isn't it?' she whispered, and saw him nod and then creep away. Vaguely she thought how it had seemed once as if it would never be daylight again, as if it would just go on getting darker and darker, more and more horrible, as if she too would soon be lost in madness. Then, she couldn't have imagined the daylight coming into the house. But it hadn't, not into that house. This was a different house.

She was very tired and sleepy, and she had to sink down and close her eyes again. But her mind went groping about and at last stumbled back through the night. It seemed different now; something had vanished from it; that huge background of nightmare, horror mounting in the dark, all that had gone. They had come running out of the rain, the black night, into this house, clamouring for shelter, and had found here some people like themselves, only twisted, crazed, with loneliness, age, some weakness of blood or brain. Their figures came swaying before her, and now for a moment she could look into each face steadily and pitifully. Last night she had been sick, terrified, despairing; to-morrow, looking back, she might be angry; but just now she could only be sorry. She thought of the five of them coming in here, saw them a long way off, dim little figures, and then vaguely tried to remember the talk they had had, what they had said. She heard Penderel's voice again. Something about a snag, the great snag. Had he got round it now, leaped over it, gone on his way? But what was it? About being taken in or being piggy, was that it? She could remember thinking it all rather young and silly, and that's all she could remember, she was so sleepy, just sorry and very sleepy.

The window showed Philip no red flares and rising ball of fire, no sudden triumph of day. It was a chill misty dawn, a landscape in smoke and steel. It held out no large promises of sunlight and the blue; yet there was a touch of kindness in its level sober light, which moved so slowly in that room to which he turned now, and dealt so gently with the eyes it found there. The morning's truth would not be proclaimed with insolent haste. It would be revealed very slowly and quietly.

As he passed, he heard a sudden little noise from Sir William, who was apparently clearing his throat. Philip stopped and turned, and saw that he was awake again. He tip-toed nearer, glancing down at Gladys, who was still in the same position, sleeping soundly. The hand above her grasped a handkerchief, tiny and crumpled. She looked like a child. Sir William looked different too in this new light, looked curiously aged, stony, desolate.

'Saw you looking out,' he told Philip in a hoarse whisper. 'What's it like?'

'The floods have gone down, I think,' Philip replied very softly. 'It's not too bad a morning.'

Sir William grunted. 'It's got plenty of time yet. Wish I could sleep.'

'I'm going to try now,' said Philip, and crept away. The next moment he was lying on the floor by the side of Margaret's chair.

'Your wife asleep?' The question came faintly.

'Yes,' he whispered, 'fast asleep.'

Lightning Source UK Ltd.
Milton Keynes UK
UKHW040735051219
354823UK00002B/430/P